W9-BKP-579

A Certain Magical Index

12

KAZUMA KAMACHI

ILLUSTRATION BY
KIYOTAKA HAIMURA

contents

"The punishment game. ♪"

Academy City
Tokiwadai Middle
School Level Five
Mikoto Misaka

"Wait, we were still on for that?"

Academy City
Level Zero
Touma Kamijou

"Ohhh..."

Nun managing the Index of Prohibited Books **Index**

"...Eh?"

Academy City's strongest Level Five **Accelerator**

《 ‥ 》

Russian Catholic
sorcerer
Sasha Kreutzev

"Archbishop!!"
English Puritan Sorcerer from Necessarius **Stiyl Magnus**
"Gyaaaaah!!"
Academy City Judgment member **Kazari Uiharu**
"Wh-wh-wha-wha-what…?!"
Archbishop of the English Puritan Church **Laura Stuart**

"B-but why, asks Mis
asks Misaka…!!"

Sisters serial number 20001
-Last Order

VOLUME 12

KAZUMA KAMACHI

ILLUSTRATION BY: KIYOTAKA HAIMURA

NEW YORK

A CERTAIN MAGICAL INDEX, Volume 12

KAZUMA KAMACHI

Translation by Andrew Prowse
Cover art by Kiyotaka Haimura

TOARU MAJYUTSU NO INDEX
©KAZUMA KAMACHI 2007
All rights reserved.
Edited by ASCII MEDIA WORKS
First published in Japan in 2007 by KADOKAWA CORPORATION, Tokyo.
English translation rights arranged with KADOKAWA CORPORATION, Tokyo,
through Tuttle-Mori Agency, Inc., Tokyo.

English translation © 2017 by Yen Press, LLC

Yen On
1290 Avenue of the Americas
New York, NY 10104

Visit us at yenpress.com
facebook.com/yenpress
twitter.com/yenpress
yenpress.tumblr.com
instagram.com/yenpress

First Yen On Edition: August 2017

Yen On is an imprint of Yen Press, LLC.
The Yen On name and logo are trademarks of Yen Press, LLC.

Library of Congress Cataloging-in-Publication Data

Names: Kamachi, Kazuma, author. | Haimura, Kiyotaka, 1973– illustrator. | Prowse, Andrew (Andrew R.), translator. | Hinton, Yoshito, translator.
Title: A certain magical index / Kazuma Kamachi ; illustration by Kiyotaka Haimura.
Other titles: To aru majyutsu no kinsho mokuroku. (Light novel). English
Description: First Yen On edition. | New York : Yen On, 2014–
Identifiers: LCCN 2014031047 (print) | ISBN 9780316339124 (v. 1 : pbk.) |
  ISBN 9780316259422 (v. 2 : pbk.) | ISBN 9780316340540 (v. 3 : pbk.) |
  ISBN 9780316340564 (v. 4 : pbk.) | ISBN 9780316340595 (v. 5 : pbk.) |
  ISBN 9780316340601 (v. 6 : pbk.) | ISBN 9780316272230 (v. 7 : pbk.) |
  ISBN 9780316359924 (v. 8 : pbk.) | ISBN 9780316359962 (v. 9 : pbk.) |
  ISBN 9780316359986 (v. 10: pbk.) | ISBN 978031636005 (v. 11: pbk.) |
  ISBN 9780316360029 (v. 12: pbk.)
Subjects: | CYAC: Magic—Fiction. | Ability—Fiction. | Nuns—Fiction. | Japan—Fiction. | Science fiction. | BISAC: FICTION / Fantasy / General. | FICTION / Science Fiction / Adventure.
Classification: LCC PZ7.1.K215 Ce 2014 | DDC [Fic]—dc23
LC record available at https://lccn.loc.gov/2014031047

ISBNs: 978-0-316-36002-9 (paperback)
978-0-316-36003-6 (ebook)

1 3 5 7 9 10 8 6 4 2

LSC-C

Printed in the United States of America

PROLOGUE

Kuroko Shirai, a Pillow, and a Bed

Suffering_of_a_Negligee.

Morning started early at Tokiwadai Middle School.

However, 5:20 AM was definitely a little too early. The birds were only just beginning to chirp at this hour, and silence normally still prevailed in the girls' dormitories. The living quarters weren't all the same. Eighty percent of the population in Academy City was students—so there were many different types and varieties of dorms. Tokiwadai, in particular, had annoyingly strict curfew and sleeping hours. (Though sometimes certain Level Fives or Judgment officers would sneak out.)

Everyone was fast asleep in the off-campus dormitories of Tokiwadai.

Except, perhaps, for Kuroko Shirai.

She tossed and turned in her bed. Awake but, more accurately, unable to sleep.

Usually she tied her brown hair into pigtails on either side, but not at that moment, so her hair was splayed across the bed. All she wore was a negligee—so thin and sheer, one would have to observe from up close to even notice she was wearing something—and short panties frilled with lace. You could see all the way from above her flat chest down to her navel, but she didn't appear bothered. Not just because this was a girls' dormitory, but because her roommate was someone special.

"…"

Abruptly, Kuroko stopped rolling around.

She looked toward the bed next to hers.

Not even fifty centimeters separated them. She was so close to the girl in that bed who was asleep, unlike Kuroko. A tiny bit of sweat clung to her shoulder-length brown hair, and her slender white fingers poked out of her baggy, light-blue pajama sleeves. She had a change of heart recently and now wore rather ornate hairpins on the side of her head, but at the moment they were sitting in a group on her nightstand.

Mikoto Misaka, Kuroko's beloved "big sister."

She was one of only seven Level Five espers in Academy City and one of just two at Tokiwadai. They called her the school ace, a monstrous middle school girl who drew ever more envy by the day. There she was, limp on her side in her bed.

"…Mm-heh-heh…have to do anything I say…punishment game…," she mumbled through her cute lips, looking incredibly happy with herself for some reason.

Shirai, in her own bed, began to madly scratch at her hair with her hands. *Gah, I need to know! What has been going on with Big Sister lately?! She's been like this ever since the Daihasei Festival!! Who in her dreams could she possibly be saying that to?!*

"Haah, haaah," she panted heavily. As their feminine names implied, Kuroko Shirai was a girl, and Mikoto Misaka was also a girl. But between them, there was something else, a girlie kind of thing, sort of like, well, you know. It would be too graphic to say it straight, so Mikoto's underclassman Kuroko had opted for the long con.

She wouldn't have a problem if Mikoto's sleep talk was directed at her. But she didn't have any recollection, at least in the past few days or so, of challenging her to a punishment game. Which meant, whether it was a boy or a girl she was talking to, this was a *huge* problem. Those were Shirai's super-individual thoughts on the situation.

Mikoto Misaka, who didn't feel any of her gloom, clutched her big pillow, the one her head was supposed to be on, in her arms.

"…What should I have you do first…mm?"

You stinking pillow!! Wh-wh-why is B-Big Sister rubbing her cheek on it now?! What is that floofy pillow supposed to represent?!

Kuroko Shirai tossed and turned in her bed, but the happy girl's eyes showed no signs of opening.

It was 5:25 AM.

And once again, she hadn't gotten enough sleep.

CHAPTER 1

The Sunny Spot During Morning Classes
Winter_Clothes.

1

September 30.

The final day of September and a half day for every school in Academy City. The reason was simple—everyone would be changing uniforms tomorrow in preparation for the colder seasons.

Academy City was large—in fact, it took up one-third of the redeveloped western areas of the Tokyo prefecture—and hosted around 1.8 million students. Even simple uniform changes sent the local clothing industry into a frenzy.

The actual measurements and ordering had been finished around the time of the Daihasei Festival, so the only thing happening today was giving newly made winter uniforms to students who didn't already have them. But despite that, the event caused large crowds, giving an idea of how uniquely massive the event was. Plus, students traditionally wore their new uniforms right away, partly to break them in.

But for students who had nothing to do with the seasonal clothing change, it was just a regular half day.

Take the boy named Touma Kamijou, for example. He'd enrolled in a certain high school this year and purchased a winter uniform back then. For him, there were no sizing issues whatsoever. No need for him to throw himself into the chaos.

It wasn't just him, either. The chaotic masses seemed to be limited to certain grades—most of the students running around like chickens with their heads cut off were second- and third-years. All the first-years were having a nice, relaxing day.

In any event, they were now on their ten-minute break between third and fourth period.

Touma Kamijou, the aforementioned average high school student, had opened a window in the hallway and was now busy staring out of it and daydreaming. Last period had been math class, and it had been so boring, he felt like he was going to die. As soon as the break started, he'd gone to the drinking fountains to wake up and wash his face.

His height and weight were average. The only thing unusual about him was maybe a bit of extra muscle on his bones. They hadn't come from any club-related physical fitness activities—they were from less healthy endeavors, like getting into fights in alleys and running away from them. His spiky black hair looked like a glimpse of a fashion magazine picture, giving an image many male high school students tended to build up with the thought of *Maybe I should make an effort to look a little nicer.* Of course, with bleary, wandering eyes and a wide-open yawning mouth, maybe his image wasn't particularly strong.

As he stood with his elbows resting on the windowsill, feeling the first cool breezes of autumn now that the summer heat was gone, he sighed and said to himself, "I hope I meet someone soon."

The moment the words left his mouth, he felt two punches thrusting into his temples from either side as though he'd been caught in a vise. There was a crazy cracking noise.

To the right of him stood Motoharu Tsuchimikado, and to the left, Blue Hair. Both were Kamijou's classmates.

"You— The heck're you doin'?!" he babbled at them, shaking his head to clear it.

Tsuchimikado looked at him, eyes glinting behind his sunglasses, not saying anything for a moment. "Nya. That sounded pretty sarcastic comin' from you, Kammy."

"I bet just your words could cause some insane lady to come tumblin' out the classroom door over there," said Blue Hair in his usual, obviously faked Osaka accent. "That's how it always is with you! Anything could appear when you're around, from super-electromagnetic robot girls to pretty nymph ladies! You've got it all!!"

When he was around, one could generally expect indecipherable gibberish. He never did it to be mean, though.

All three of them wore black vests with stand-up collars and black slacks. Kamijou's vest was unbuttoned, showing the red T-shirt he wore underneath. Students normally wore button-down shirts underneath, of course, but Tsuchimikado had hair dyed blond and Blue Hair wore necklaces. The school didn't care about the dress code too much.

"Anyway, what do the two of you want?"

"Yo, that's right! Check this out," said Blue Hair, thrusting a manga magazine—the most popular in the country—into Kamijou's face.

What a good friend. He hadn't used it to hit him.

Blue Hair flipped the magazine over, revealing a color advertisement for mail-order goods. "Check it! Mr. Shoulder Massage, see?"

"Yeah, and?"

"Sounds cool, huh? My right shoulder's been achin' the last few days. And when I tried to rub my own shoulder, my *left* shoulder started to hurt."

"Hey, this is the one they were doing those late-night infomercials on."

"I know, right?! It's super friggin' crazy! This shoulder massage machine takes up, like, the whole back page, so it's gotta feel so good!!"

"Huh," said Tsuchimikado suspiciously. "They're probably exaggerating. You can't put real numbers on how good something feels, nya. Aren't they basically sayin' *all the testers felt real good, but hey, who knows, right*?"

"Geh! You have your stepsister rub 'em every day! You wouldn't understand!!"

"Not every day! Maybe like once every three days, nya!!"

This all sounded like the usual small talk. Especially how Blue

Hair later claimed that something had changed the topic. Kamijou wondered what they wanted him for.

The two responded to his thoughts.

"Anyway, Kammy, what do you think? I think it's gotta be good stuff for sure."

"I, for one, don't think it'll have you crying out in joy, nya."

Kamijou sighed. They just wanted a third opinion to break the tie. Why were they so fixated on this shoulder-rubbing machine, anyway? "You know, I'm not a massage specialist or anything. My opinion doesn't mean much. One of you might have a majority, but what would be the point?"

"Sheesh, why do you have to be so freaking useless?!"

"Don't call me useless!!" he shot back on reflex, finally realizing they were just trying to fire him up. He let them do it, though. That was how verbal conflicts started. "I don't really think it does much. Everyone gets knots in their shoulders, but they all hurt differently and in different places. And wouldn't it be less effective for one gender than another? They're pretty much announcing that this is the miracle we've all been waiting for to relax our shoulders, so it's a little fishy, I guess."

"I told you, nya. Stepsisters are the best cure for shoulder cramps."

"You can't say that without actually doing science!" protested Blue Hair. "Besides, I don't have a girl to rub my shoulders! That's why I'm having this problem in the first place!!"

He and Tsuchimikado started showering each other with blows. As Kamijou watched the fruitless conflict develop, he decided to offer a third perspective. "Well," he said, peeling them away from each other. "Why don't we put it to the test for real? I happen to know just the right person—one who gets shoulder pains *and* has a huge weakness for mail-order products."

2

One of the students in Touma Kamijou's class was named Seiri Fukiyose.

She had a strong sense of responsibility, and she'd been working on the Daihasei Festival executive committee until just a few days ago. Her black hair was tucked behind her ears, and her chest was on the large side for a student. She gave off the impression that she was fussy about rules and regulations—a textbook and a notebook were already out on her desk despite the class still being on break. She wore a long-sleeved sailor uniform, and aside from her skirt being a bit short, everything from her scarf to her slippers was measured and standardized.

She also found it fun to collect mail-order health products. Possibly due to a complex about it, nobody knew about her hobby...aside from a certain boy.

She was in her seat, not in any rush to compare homework or notes with others, making idle conversation with the classmate who sat next to her, Aisa Himegami, when...

"Is Fukiyose in there?!"

Bang!! The classroom door had barely opened before a shout from that direction made her flinch. The ones asking after her were the Idiot Delta Force of their class—Kamijou, Blue Hair, and Tsuchimikado. They'd caused all sorts of problems in the past, and Fukiyose had sworn to herself she would remain calm no matter what happened when dealing with these three.

Kamijou, though, had other ideas.

"I'll never ask you for anything else ever, Fukiyose! Let me have a rub!!"

The big-breasted girl heard a single, strange *crack* in her mind.

Before the word *calm* could even reach her brain, she'd already intercepted the charging Motoharu Tsuchimikado and Blue Hair with straight punches and rattled Touma Kamijou in that hard forehead of his as he grimaced at seeing the other two get mowed down. She looked down at the villains writhing on the floor and dusted herself off before their 135-centimeter-tall female teacher, Komoe Tsukuyomi, entered the room.

"Okay, everyone! I'll be teaching you chemistry for today's last class, and…Gyaaahhh?! A lawless battle between delinquents?! Is this what my peaceful class has transformed into?!"

"It was for the sake of peace."

"What in the world happened? Fuki, you're acting like you're part of a peacekeeping brigade!!"

Komoe almost sounded like she was crying. From the floor, Kamijou let out a groan and said, "M-Ms. Komoe…Nobody did anything wrong, really…"

"Then why did this happen?!" Komoe cried.

Kamijou raised a shaky finger at somewhere a little below Seiri Fukiyose's face. "…It's just, Fukiyose's got stuff that feels really good, and she won't let us have even a little rub!!"

That was enough for Komoe to blush fiercely and fall over backward. Fukiyose didn't check on her—instead she clenched her fist and slowly moved in to continue her assault.

3

Four girls stood in a hospital.

Their location was far from the routes connecting the entrance to the hospital rooms, so while it wasn't intended to be off-limits, it was still usually empty. The hospital had designated this section a "clinical research area," a pompous name considering all the warm sunlight streaming in from the windows.

They were in a hallway.

All four had brown, shoulder-length hair and clear, pale complexions. Their silhouettes were exactly alike and each bore the same eyes—in shape, color, pupils, and retinas. They all wore gray pleated skirts, white short-sleeved blouses, and sleeveless summer sweaters, the slightly out-of-season summer uniform of Tokiwadai Middle School.

They went by many names.

The Sisters.

Radio Noise.

Military mass-production model Level Fives.

These girls had shortened life spans thanks to genetic manipulation and drug-induced growth stimulation technology. They were here at the hospital now to solve that problem through many treatments. The second phase had begun just today. Until now, they'd been cloistered away in hospital beds, but their rehabilitation now involved small, frequent trips outside.

A doctor with a face like a frog, holding a small clipboard similar to the kind a waiter might carry, spoke to the Sisters. "So? Would you have rather worn Tokiwadai winter uniforms outside?"

"There is no problem, replies Misaka number 10032," asserted one of the four. They were differentiated not by name, but by their serial numbers. The frog-faced doctor wasn't the one who made that decision; all he knew was that it had been decided when they were manufactured.

"Are all four of you the same size?" he asked, jotting down an order request on his clipboard.

The four Sisters didn't even exchange glances. They all made a face, like the answer was obvious.

"You needn't measure us all individually, as we all match, answers Misaka number 10032."

"All Misakas are mass-production models created from the same genes, adds Misaka number 13577."

"This is how we were made, so you need not think about differences in size, concludes Misaka number 10039."

"I...Well...," the last one stammered.

""""...?"""""

The three other Sisters turned to the fourth upon hearing her trouble.

Misaka number 19090 looked away and cringed a little. She seemed to be trying to cover her upper chest with her hands.

Number 10032—called Little Misaka by a certain young man—gave her the slightest strange look before appearing to have an epiphany.

She approached number 19090. Then she clenched her fists, stuck out her thumbs, turned her fists upside down, and plunged those two fingers straight between number 19090's skirt and body.

"What?! She should be exactly as the specifications suggest, yet there are two full thumb widths of space here, reports Misaka number 10032 immediately!!"

"Every Misaka should be the same Misaka, cries Misaka number 13577 in shock!"

"If the waist is different, what about everything else? asks Misaka number 10039, proposing a detailed examination with a completely calm attitude."

At the proposal, number 10032 removed her fingers from number 19090's skirt and brought them upward. Number 19090 used both her hands to intercept them. It seemed like she had more colorful, vivid emotions than the others—her face was becoming a little red.

The frog-faced doctor shook his head. "Even monozygotic twins end up having different faces and bodies based on differences in what they eat or how much they exercise, all right? It's not very strange that one in a group of clones would end up having a good figure."

The doctor had been privately regretting a statement from earlier that he shouldn't have made. Ever since he'd taught them that thinner women are considered better by men and thus more likely to be chosen by them, they'd been like this. That was all his personal, biased taste. Unfortunately, the Sisters had extremely few male acquaintances and considered him an archetypical male. They seemed to have concluded thusly: "If this man says so, then would *that high school student* think so as well? murmurs Misaka in deep thought."

Also, they'd been acting under the impression—and he didn't know where they'd learned this—that there existed in the world a special ring to put on one's ring finger, and to acquire it, one needed to be "good" in all respects. He couldn't decide whether they were right or wrong about that, but because of it, individuality had unexpectedly began blooming within the Sisters. (They didn't seem to be very aware of it themselves.)

"Which means this one has been secretly on a diet and not telling us, says Misaka number 10032, pursuing the question."

"Number 20001, Last Order, who unifies all Misakas—what was she doing? asks Misaka number 13577, suggesting the words *duty* and *responsibility*."

"That tiny shrimp may not have understood the significance of her actions, speculates Misaka number 10039, not losing her composure."

As each of them spoke to one another without regard for the frog-faced doctor, he put a word in. "I don't think it's anything to get that excited about, hmm? You're all identical parts of a whole, so if you do the same thing as number 19090 there, you should see the same changes, too."

"«««...!!»»»"

Wpshh!! The three Sisters whipped around to face the remaining one.

Number 19090, who had acquired the "slim figure" skill a step ahead of the rest, backed away slowly. "Misaka will now flee the scene in accordance with her crisis control capabilities, says Misa...!!"

Before her shout ended, the other girls attacked.

4

Inside the same hospital where the Sisters were raging, there was a woman named Kikyou Yoshikawa.

She was a former member of the research group that had planned and implemented an "experiment" to try to create a new Level Six esper classification to top the existing rankings in Academy City that ranged from Level Zero up to Level Five.

She thought of her personality not as kind, but as soft—and during the experiment, she had created twenty thousand human clones in total and killed half of them throughout the trial. A certain Level Five student, the Level Six "Absolute" candidate, had done the actual deed, but of course, that was no excuse.

The experiment had been labeled fatally flawed and was not only frozen, but fully suspended.

That didn't mean, though, that everything related to the experiment had vanished into thin air overnight. The girls who had been created only to be killed and the esper who had been ordered only to kill them…They may have come from special environments and had unique physical characteristics, but they were all still human children. The mental pressure on them defied imagination. Their individual problems were one thing, but a large rift sat between them, and their relationship was essentially catastrophic at best. Thinking normally, they couldn't possibly form anything even resembling a bond.

And yet…

"Nooo! refuses Misaka refuses Misaka! I'm not getting off, I won't! This duffel bag is now Misaka's base! says Misaka says Misaka, sitting formally on her knees atop the bag you're holding and arguing firmly!!"

"You…!! Can't you see I'm trying to hold this thing, you brat?! Quit playing around on it!! You didn't forget the fact that I'm still recovering, did you?"

But here we have two such people, and they're as energetic as ever, thought Yoshikawa.

The "killer"—called Accelerator—held a modern crutch in his right hand like a tonfa and a duffel bag strap on his left shoulder as he tilted to and fro. His uniquely colorless, white hair and red eyes. Right now, he wore mostly gray clothing.

The "victim"—called Last Order—perched atop Accelerator's duffel bag while sitting on the soles of her feet, each hand on one of its straps like she was on a swing, which she could do because she looked like she was about ten years old. Still, for someone on a crutch, it might have hurt. She had brown hair down to her shoulders, brown eyes, and wore a sky-blue camisole and a men's button-down, which hung off her, the sleeves far too long for her arms.

Accelerator had been hospitalized after being shot in the forehead on August 31. A month later, they'd finally given him permission to leave the hospital. Not because his body had healed, strictly speaking, but because they'd done all the treatment he needed. He hadn't escaped the aftereffects of his brain injury caused by the broken fragments of his skull, but he'd regained some function via a choker-like electrode he wore around his neck even now. Without it, he wouldn't be able to speak. He wouldn't even be able to stand upright by himself. Still, given how severe the injury had been, simply being able to return to his daily life was a miracle.

That was the current situation as they stood at the hospital entrance.

Yoshikawa had actually taken a grazing bullet to the heart herself, so she wasn't in the best condition to look after children. She'd taken on the role anyway.

Not because she had to—because she wanted to.

"All right, all right. You're going to bother people if you play in the entrance. Let's leave that for after we get our things settled."

"Misaka wasn't playing! she argues with a serious face, pushing her center of gravity down some more!!"

"If this pulling sort of entertainment isn't 'playing,' then what the hell is it?!" shouted Accelerator, about to be crushed by the duffel bag.

Without listening, Yoshikawa walked a short distance away from the entrance and gave the taxi driver she had waiting for them a casual wave. With slow, practiced motions, the passenger car approached.

Accelerator lifted the luggage with Last Order on it to the driver. "I'm throwing everything into the trunk, so open it. Now."

"You're treating Misaka like luggage?! says Misaka says Misaka, trembling and fleeing into the backseat!!"

Accelerator tossed the duffel bag into the backseat, which crushed Last Order with a yelp, then sat down in the empty space.

The backseat had room for more people, but Yoshikawa wasn't about to let herself get wrapped up in their quarreling and took the passenger-side seat instead.

Just to be sure, she told the driver, "They were discharged recently, so they're worked up right now."

"Ah-ha-ha. Isn't it better for children to be energetic?"

"Also, the smaller one isn't used to cars, so she may throw up."

"?!" The driver visibly twitched.

Must be new, noted Yoshikawa offhandedly. She heard rustling, which told her Accelerator had taken his bag and gotten away from Last Order. She'd actually lied but complaining about it would just make the ride smoother. Her underhanded trick didn't seem to have major effects, though the taxi's start was so smooth it was like the driver thought he was carrying unbroken eggs.

Yoshikawa told the driver their destination, then checked the digital clock above the meter. It was nearly noon.

Accelerator, who believed the bit about throwing up, caught Last Order's face as she got closer to him and pushed her away. He cast a dubious look at the back of Yoshikawa's head. "Where're we going?"

"To a school where a friend of mine works. We're meeting her there. You'll have to quit your current school, right? You know what that means."

Most students who lived in Academy City used dormitories. A few lived rent-free at bread shops and the like, but such cases were extremely rare.

In this city, leaving the school system (more accurately, the Ability Development agencies, some of which were schools) also meant losing residency at one's dormitory. Accelerator, constantly targeted by Academy City delinquents who'd made a mess out of his dorm room, had no attachment to where he lived. It wasn't worth anything now, either, since they hadn't left a single piece of furniture unbroken. Still, having the roof over his head stolen from him was a pretty major occurrence.

Accelerator had chosen to quit his school despite all the risks, because "...I'll pass on being part of any of this Level Six bullshit, thanks."

True, the agencies directly involved in the experiment had gone under—but even if the research facilities that used the Sisters had gone away, the spell hadn't been lifted. His school, like others, had a "special class," though on a much smaller scale. He was the only student in the classroom, that animal cage where they practically cordoned him off like a lab rat.

If he was going to leave that bloody (in every sense of the word) world behind him, he needed to abandon everything he'd known until now. The laboratory, his school, his dormitory—everything.

This time he'd just have to choose a new place that didn't want to do all that. Accelerator was an attractive research subject. He didn't know if there were any researchers who wouldn't bat an eye at him, but he had to try.

Accelerator and Last Order were far too extraordinary to find a place to be outside Academy City. And unless he participated in the Academy City school system, Accelerator would have to live like the armed back-alley Level Zero organization, Skill-Out. If the strongest Level Five in Academy City started down that road, only total destruction awaited.

He made a twisted grin. "So, you'll be in charge of me now. That the General Board's decision? Seems just right for you, in a research sorta way."

Yoshikawa had once been on the experiment's research team. She'd done maintenance on the clone production, including Last Order, and also took care of Accelerator's needs.

Even with the Level Six–related research suspended, he was still the strongest Level Five esper in Academy City and an excellent specimen. If he had Yoshikawa study him and the findings were used in new Ability Development tech…Well, there was a lot of money in it.

It didn't matter how far he went. He would always feel subject to someone else's expectations, someone else's influence.

Still, most of the people Accelerator had met in the past could be described as "off the rails." Considering his newfound freedom from their curse, Accelerator giving Yoshikawa authority over his actions would probably make things easier for him. And of course, if he didn't like how she did things, he could always crush her and look for someone else.

But…

"That's not quite right," said Kikyou Yoshikawa suddenly, without turning around.

"Eh?"

"I'm not your next supervisor. Calm down and think about it. Right now, I, Kikyou Yoshikawa, am no longer a researcher, and I'm on a razor's edge when it comes to employment. Plus, I got involved in not one, but *two* incidents centering on you: the experiment and what happened August thirty-first. If the General Board thinks I should be your guardian now, I'd want them all fired."

"…So what, exactly? You just wipin' their asses for them now? Bet you're handing us over to some researcher we don't know."

"So paranoid. Makes sense given your living environment, though. Let me point out two mistakes in your speculation. First, I plan to hand you over to someone you already know. Second, she's no researcher."

"…" Accelerator narrowed his eyes and mulled over what she'd said.

He couldn't trust her. He would have felt better if this brat sitting next to him wasn't here, but even with her weighing him down, he could crush any opponents who came at him. It also seemed quicker to meet with the person and deal "politely" with them rather than needing to stay vigilant for a long time expecting would-be assailants. *Looks like this is gonna get real boring.*

And then Last Order, in her perfect innocence, said without a care in the world, "I don't think I know anyone who's not a researcher except Yomikawa, suggests Misaka says Misaka, raising her hand."

"That's correct," answered Yoshikawa happily.

Yomikawa was one of Kikyou Yoshikawa's few friends in the above-the-table world, as it were. She worked as an Anti-Skill officer in Academy City. Ever since Yoshikawa had been hospitalized because of her bullet wound, the tracksuit-wearing woman had been dropping by every now and then to look after Accelerator and Last Order.

Accelerator swore to himself. He hadn't considered the possibility until she said it.

Yoshikawa heard him and asked, "Goodness. You know the right answers for the test, and you're still nervous?"

"...You know, I could just *politely* force the answers out of you right now."

"Well, you'll know if I'm lying when we get there. Your habit of being cautious when other people say nice things to you is one you want to keep, I think. Especially if you knew how much what you're protecting is worth."

He couldn't stand Yoshikawa. Accelerator looked away from the passenger's seat and cast a resentful glare out the car window. Only Last Order didn't seem to have noticed their exchange, as she went on saying, "Huh? Is it not Yomikawa? asks Misaka asks Misaka, tugging on your shoulders."

5

Afternoon happened, so school ended.

Kamijou didn't have any particular club activities to do, so the only thing left for him was to return home to his dorm.

After going to the lockers and putting his shoes on, he plodded toward the exit of the school grounds, saying to himself, "I wonder what I did wrong."

He was thinking, of course, about how the massage machine and Seiri Fukiyose's head-butt were connected.

Hmm. Maybe "Let me have a rub, Fukiyose!!" was a bit too informal? But then I said, "Please let me get a rub, O great and powerful Fukiyose," and she got angry. And then I started with, "Dear Fukiyose, I hope this letter finds you enjoying the deepening colors of autumn...," and she came at me with a full-on head-butt. What'd I do to offend her?

The boy was basically used to misfortune befalling him. Even when things got physical, his body could take random attacks like that. He was proud of it, but that meant he really didn't have any adhesive plaster for his wounds. A hungry girl bit him in the head on a daily basis, after all. His endurance was nothing to sneeze at.

Without realizing the fundamental problem, he went on thinking at length—things like *Maybe I should have chosen a more nonchalant way of opening the letter*, as he walked through Academy City's neat and tidy streets.

The last of summer's lingering heat was completely gone now that it was September 30. The gentle breeze turning the wind turbine propellers as well as the big-screen TV weather forecasts plastered to department store walls indicating no need for air conditioners anymore both morphed the citywide message of "Be careful of heat stroke" to "Seasons are changing, so watch your health."

Meanwhile—

"Found it, the terrible piece of crap you are!"

The girl's words rushed at him as if to clearly demonstrate a linguist critic's opinion that spoken Japanese grew more disorderly by the day.

He turned to look just as a fair young lady (at least, she should have been) from a famed girls' school called Tokiwadai Middle School finished quickly stomping up to him.

Mikoto Misaka.

She had brown, shoulder-length hair and was about seven centimeters shorter than him. Unlike her previous summer uniform, she now wore a beige blazer and a dark-blue checkered, pleated skirt. They'd just gotten their sparkly new winter uniforms, and her skirt was even shorter now. And befitting a "proper young lady," not only did she carry her schoolbag, but also an instrument case, possibly holding a violin.

Kamijou made a sour face as soon as he saw her. "Huh? Well, this is…you know. What rotten luck!"

"You can't say that to someone as soon as you see them!!" Mikoto yelled back.

Incidentally, Kamijou had already gotten a punch and a head-butt from Seiri Fukiyose this morning. But this bad luck's impact was sure to be stronger. It was only natural—this so-called "Railgun" girl had been regularly shooting electric spears and things of that nature at him for a long while now.

Kamijou hefted his cheap schoolbag as though it weighed a ton. "Anyway, what do you want? And keep it short. And let's walk at the same time. Actually, can I just go home now?"

"Your initial reaction was already irritating, but now you're really piling it on..." Mikoto tilted her head a little bit as her lips began to twist into a mean smile. "Wait, do you think you're in a position right now to completely mouth off to me like that?"

"Eh?"

Kamijou caught on to something evil from her level words. He tried to slowly back away from her.

Then, the ace of Tokiwadai, a proper young lady of good conduct (or else there'd be a problem), folded her arms and intoned three words:

"The punishment game. ♪"

Touma Kamijou's eyebrow twitched.

The punishment game concerned a bet he and Mikoto had made during the Daihasei Festival. All of Academy City participated in this big athletic meet that had taken place the week of September 19. Simply put, whoever got the lower ranking had to do what the other said.

As Academy City was the city for supernatural Ability Development, the rules allowed students to use their powers during the festival. Tokiwadai Middle School had mowed down the other schools' students wholesale with lances made of million-volt electrical currents, squalls rushing forward at eighty meters per second, and the like. Their tactics had been nothing short of natural disasters.

Kamijou was in high school and Mikoto in middle school, but the age difference didn't matter whatsoever. On the third day of the festival, those disasters beat him to a pulp after a direct confrontation. On top of that, Kamijou, Tsuchimikado, Himegami, and

Fukiyose had already been injured during some trouble on opening day. Everything ended up overlapping, and Kamijou suffered a conclusive defeat. His school's overall ranking was horrible, too. Given the situation, there was nothing they could have done against Tokiwadai.

But a loss was a loss.

Mikoto Misaka's punishment game was legitimate according to proper procedure.

"Wait, we were still on for that?"

"Don't start trying to bury the hatchet on your own!! Anyway, I really am going to make you do whatever I say! Hah, you should be thankful I was kind enough to wait until now without adding interest!!" Mikoto stuck out her chest, needlessly proud of her victory.

The other students on the main road were starting to look at them, wondering what was going on.

Based on Mikoto's exaggerated reaction, she had likely wanted to do this earlier, but then Kamijou wound up in the hospital and then jetted off to Italy and stuff, neglecting her. Now her resentment had culminated in a fine explosion. He was about to say, *You wouldn't call this interest?* but decided to act like an adult and stay quiet.

"Well, whatever. I guess I'm fine with it. Don't think there's gonna be very much I can do for you, though."

"Hmm. So that's how you're going to try to weasel out of this."

"No, that's not what I—"

"I get it. You're just an average person, so there's not much you can do, hmm? Oh, well, that's perfectly fine. Unlike you, I, the wonderful Mikoto, made sure to take that into consideration. I won't request anything an idiot can't do. But even average people can put in the hard work while they're complaining, right?"

"…"

Kamijou heard a strange *crack* come from his temple.

This wasn't leading anywhere good. Unfortunately, he wasn't a good enough student to be calm about it. "Fine," he said offhandedly, eyes downcast.

For some reason, Mikoto breathed a sigh of relief.

However.

All of a sudden, his down-turned face shot up to fire a level stare at her. Rallying all the strength he could muster, he said:

"Very well, then!! You may ask whatever you like of your pet slave, Touma Kamijou!!"

The people around them all froze. They looked between Kamijou the speaker and Mikoto the listener, then started whispering among themselves. Within seconds, the throng pulled away from the two of them like a raging wave.

"Uh...? What—a slave...? Huh?! What the heck are you talking about?!"

He saw the blood drain from Mikoto's face no less quickly, but his parents didn't raise him to be soft enough to grant forgiveness just for that.

Kamijou fell to his knees in a respectful pose, took out a thin writing board from his raggedy schoolbag, and, his face serious, without even the slightest trace of joking, began fanning her with it. "We'll start from the basics, my lady: making your environment comfortable. I, the humble Touma Kamijou, am ill-versed in such things, so this may take some effort on my part, but I humbly ask for your esteemed forgiveness in this regard."

"You—idiot!! That turnaround was way too fast! And don't fan me that hard from under my skirt!!"

Mikoto's pale face quickly flushed red as she shouted, holding her already short skirt down. She was wearing short pants underneath anyway, but it seemed like it was more of an emotional problem.

Just then...

"Big Sisteeer!!"

As the crowd collectively cringed, a girl wearing a blazer and twin tails burst forth.

"What...What is this?!"

Normally, this newcomer probably would have glomped Mikoto

or at least grabbed her hands, but today, for whatever reason, she reeled backward like she'd bounced off an invisible wall separating her from Mikoto. The scene must have been pretty shocking.

"K-Kuroko?"

Mikoto, who had made an older man grovel before her in public and fan her (or that's what it looked like, anyway), moved only her head to face her underclassman, her expression drawn back into a wince.

Kuroko Shirai didn't seem to hear her beloved "big sister" speak. Her tiny body began to tremble. She fixed her stare on Touma Kamijou, who had transformed into a lowly, loyal servant (or that's what it looked like, anyway).

She spoke. "Wh-what a beautifully clean posture of subordination...But that role should belong to me and me alone!"

In Shirai's eyes were envy, jealousy, and a tiny bit of reverence.

"Stop, you morons!! Don't you both start bowing to me like that! Is this some kind of ritual?! I don't remember becoming the founder of some weird religious cult!!"

Despite Mikoto Misaka's yell, Touma Kamijou didn't divert any of his attention away from his mindless fanning, while Kuroko Shirai, having reconfirmed the presence of a powerful rival, simply continued to tremble.

6

In the faculty room, Komoe Tsukuyomi heaved a worn-out sigh.

The display of exhaustion didn't quite suit her 135-centimeter frame and her resemblance to a twelve-year-old, but there was no helping it. The violent incident among her students during the morning had been harrowing (yes, it might not have been too remarkable, considering the fact that Kamijou was involved, but in terms of a normal student's life, this would have been considered a fairly big problem), but there was another factor.

And it was strewn all over her steel desktop.

Sheets of cheap paper with the words *Future Plans Survey* printed on them. Doing this survey with first-years meant their plans would be vague for the most part, though, so it was no different from a "What do you want to do when you grow up?" questionnaire. Teachers were still far from attacking the students with the regular questions—whether they would continue their education at a university after graduation or enter the workforce, what school they'd try to get into in the case of the former or what company they'd seek employment at in the case of the latter.

"Haaah…" She cradled her head in her hands.

Tsuchimikado had written, in extremely serious handwriting, that he wanted to go "to the land of maids, incite a coup, become their tactician, and raise one unfortunate maid into an empress." Blue Hair had written the words "I want to be popular" so large that they went outside the box allotted for them. Touma Kamijou, for his part, "just wanted to be happy," and he "didn't care how," an earnest, somewhat tear-jerking wish.

I've heard experts discussing how today's youth lack passion for actual jobs, but I don't think this is what they were talking about!

If they had simply wanted to avoid doing the assignment and let their mechanical pencils do all the writing, that would be one thing. But it was very plausible that they were totally serious. That's why their answers were troubling on more than one level.

That was when a female teacher in a tracksuit walked in.

"Yo, Teach. Time for a change of pace—you want cigs or alcohol?"

"We're not allowed to drink on the job, you know…"

Normally Komoe would have shouted that and launched into an explanation on something, but today she was pretty tired. She spoke flatly, too.

Yomikawa's eyes darted across Komoe's desk. "Cigs it is, then. 'Kay?"

Komoe took a cigarette out of the proffered box and put it in her mouth. "Huh? This feels sort of expensive."

"Well, it's something I got from that new cigarette bar that opened. High-quality cigs. They cost seventy yen a pop."

Nowadays, with smoking areas expanding, smoking-specific establishments had begun cropping up and gaining ground. Bars featuring cigarettes from around the world instead of cocktails weren't rare. Seventy yen for one wasn't much considering some had three-thousand-yen cigars made in South America.

Most schools were designated entirely nonsmoking, but a surprising number in Academy City permitted cigarettes inside the building. The reasoning was that many schoolteachers were also researchers involved in various fields, and the Academy City General Board considered impairing their focus to be a detriment to the whole city. Therefore, if a teacher requested permission to smoke, the board supplied them with small, high-efficiency atmospheric scrubbers. Komoe opened the drawer of her steel desk, then took out four such devices, each with about two boxes of cigarettes stored inside. She positioned one at each of her desk's four corners.

Each could only absorb air from one direction. With four operating at once, they would move in a circular pattern around her desk like a churning washing machine. The flow of air was so subtle it wouldn't even move a flimsy sheet of paper, but it would catch all the cigarette smoke and absorb it, run it through a filter, and spit out clean air.

These were the latest models, utilizing the principles of aerodynamics in their design. What's more, the developers had succeeded in driving the cost down to the point where the devices could be distributed for free. A practical consumer good in every sense of the term.

"There," said Komoe, switching the air purifiers at the edges of her desk on.

The unbelievably big-breasted teacher in the green tracksuit, Aiho Yomikawa, placed a cigarette in her own mouth, then lit it with a small lighter from Komoe's desk. "Apparently, they're rare ones from Belgium…Yuck. This is a failure. I just can't seem to understand the subtler flavors."

"That's because you don't take the time to savor each one. You just smoke whole boxes at a time. It's dulled your senses!"

"So says the White Smoker, Ms. Komoe, famous for smoking five times the amount I do in a single day."

Both of them loudly puffed out smoke toward the desk's surface.

The white haze that hit the tabletop scattered about but stopped at its four edges as though blocked by an invisible wall. Then the vapors began swirling around before those four corners eventually sucked them in.

The air purifiers only worked properly on desks like this. This wasn't a problem for Komoe, since she was sitting in her chair, but Yomikawa had to lean forward to get her face closer to the desk. In that sense, there was still room for improvement.

"It looks like cigarette prices are going up. I'm so disappointed!"

"They're still cheaper than pastries and comic books, though."

Eighty percent of Academy City's population was students. Even excluding college students, there were surprisingly few inhabitants allowed to smoke tobacco or imbibe alcoholic beverages. The reality was that taxing them wouldn't do much to bolster the city's finances. Instead, the city quietly acquiesced to levying taxes on things children enjoyed.

This city was essentially a place for studying, and the trend of the times was willingly taxing nonessential products and luxuries. But the average dormitory rent and meal expenses (though some meals were Academy City "trial products") were incredibly low, so it all evened out in the end. Of course, some schools did profit off school buses, class materials, and the like.

"But most students get their living stipend from scholarships and subsidies supplied by Academy City, yeah? Still seems like a roundabout way of doing things, if you ask me."

"If the authorities directly reduced scholarships, they'd be flooded with complaints. The money's going to the same place, but the methods get different reactions. Kind of like whether they say they're taxing cigarettes or lowering our salaries."

"I guess so," said Yomikawa, fishing a portable ashtray out of her tracksuit pocket and tapping the ashes from her cigarette into it.

And then she realized something.

The corners of Komoe's lips were turning up and down with the cigarette in her mouth, making it wiggle. That was a new habit.

"Heh. Did you learn that from the smoking priest you told me about, Teach?"

Komoe's shoulders gave a massive start. Flustered, she moved the cigarette back to the center of her lips. "N-no, I didn't! You're being absolutely ridiculous all of a sudden, Ms. Yomikawa! I would never pick up on his habits or anything! That's just crazy!!"

"Well, all right, then," said Yomikawa, giving up right then and there. Komoe had fully assumed a defensive position.

The small-statured teacher seemed to deflate at the anticlimactic development, but her expression revealed the truth. She grumbled, still wary.

Yomikawa took another pull from her cigarette. "Anyway, I should get going."

"Oh, Ms. Yomikawa, are the children you talked about coming soon?"

"You got it. They come from some troubled backgrounds, but, well...I don't mind if they're a little stupid. My class is full of over-achievers. It's totally boring."

"Oh, wait! My cigarette still has a while to go. Please, let me smoke it just a little bit longer!" cried Komoe, grabbing Yomikawa's hand. Basically, everywhere but the faculty room was nonsmoking.

A few minutes later, Komoe, who had smoked the entire cigarette right in front of the filters, followed the tracksuit-clad teacher out of the room.

7

He heard an engine sound as the taxi behind him drove away.

He didn't watch.

Next to him, Last Order was saying something, but he didn't look at her, either.

His eyes were glued to the strange scene unfolding in front of him.

In a bit more detail, they were near the school gate of a certain high school. Even from far away, the reinforced concrete school building was utterly normal and average, with nothing about it standing out.

That wasn't the problem.

Accelerator wasn't looking at the school building.

In front of them were two women who claimed they taught at this school.

He knew one of them.

It was the woman in the green tracksuit, her long hair tied back. She was Aiho Yomikawa or something like that. She was also an Anti-Skill officer in the city. She claimed to have no interest in pointing weapons at children, so she always went up against Level Three espers and below with nothing but a shield. A lunatic gym teacher.

She wasn't the problem.

Accelerator had his eyes fixed on the other person.

"Wh-what is it…?"

The woman introduced herself as Komoe Tsukuyomi…but she almost looked even smaller than Last Order, who was once again sitting formally on top of his duffel bag.

Accelerator thought for a moment, cast a glance at the extremely short woman, and said, "What's this unidentified creature for? How did she sneak into the city?"

"I didn't sneak in. I graduated from a university the normal way and came here."

That only made him more confused. He narrowed his eyes. "Then this must mean the tech that halts cell aging is finished, eh? What a load of bullshit. Guess you're one of those two-hundred-fifty-year-olds they were whispering about during the experiment. And here I thought I'd seen it all. How far has this city's research gone, anyway…?!"

"U-um, no, that's not…"

"Or maybe the technology isn't finished yet, and she's a biosample they captured to analyze, says Misaka says Misaka in an earnest tone of voice…That's terrible. I bet she's a part of so many experiments she never ever has any free time anymore, says Misaka says Misaka with a handkerchief in one hand and stuff."

"Excuse me! All I did was introduce myself. Why are you being so severe about this?! Ms. Yomikawa, stop laughing! Please do something about them!!"

The woman in the tracksuit held her gut while she laughed at the fidgeting mini-teacher. Even Kikyou Yoshikawa, who had brought Accelerator and Last Order here, probably hadn't expected Yomikawa to have a companion like this. She was smiling, too, but in a dangerous way, like a scientist who just found something new to research.

Yomikawa, still amused, looked at Accelerator. "Anyway, I'll be looking after the two of you from now on, 'kay? I have an extra room anyway, so don't hesitate to freeload."

"…This is only temporary, got it?" Accelerator replied, not amused.

In response, Komoe asked, "D-did you clear up the misunderstanding?" as Yomikawa started cheerfully knocking her on the head.

"Are you even okay with this?" Accelerator inquired, his inflection unaccountably calm. "You know about all the shit going on with me. If you think the worst that'll happen is grenades thrown at you in the middle of the night, you're naïve. Protect me, and you make all the ugliest parts of the city your enemy."

"That's exactly why," Yomikawa said, also speaking as though everything was routine. "Did you forget what I do for a living? As an Anti-Skill officer, it actually makes things easier for me, yeah? 'Sides, I don't think anyone would be stupid enough to attack an Anti-Skill officer's house. It's the dark side of the city, which means we're not supposed to see it. If they declare war like that, they know which one of us'll be the last ones standing."

"…" Accelerator paused as he thought about that.

Only Komoe seemed confused as she looked around saying, "Huh? When did the mood change so much?"

"Don't come cryin' to me if you die," he said.

"Oh, it'll be fine," Yomikawa insisted.

"You might even get your name on *their* list."

"My job's to rehabilitate delinquent groups like that. I need to save them; can't compromise with 'em if I'm scared."

Accelerator sucked his teeth in annoyance.

First, Last Order, now her. When did idiots like them start wanting to be around him? He felt like he was totally out of place here, all by himself.

In spite of Accelerator's sour face, Yomikawa grinned in an unladylike fashion. "Still, this is good. You'll be easier to save than I heard."

"You fuckin' serious?"

Yomikawa was probably talking about whether she could rehabilitate him.

She had no way of knowing, but Accelerator was already directly involved in the deaths of over ten thousand people. Knowing that fact made it clear to him how little sense Yomikawa's words made.

However—

Aiho Yomikawa, without realizing it, continued to speak to him. "I mean, come on. You say all that, but after you heard you'd be living with me, you went down a checklist, trying to make sure there were no blind spots. Trying to close up even the smallest holes so that we wouldn't get attacked if worse came to worst. That means you're all fired up to protect us, eh?"

"…" Accelerator frowned deeply. *This is why I can't handle people like these idiots*, he thought to himself. *They can't get a grip on the situation.*

8

For the time being, Kamijou split up with Mikoto Misaka.

The reasons were simple—he was hungry, he wanted to change out of his sweaty school uniform, and unless he cooked for himself, he wouldn't be able to deal with the huge mountain of thin, wheat flour noodles he now had. He didn't know if the dry *soumen* had an expiration date, but in a mental sort of way, he wanted to avoid having this year's noodles carry over into the next one.

Mikoto had shouted, "Who cares about some stupid noodles?!" but when Kamijou, with excessive determination, shouted back, "Then how would you like to try having to eat *soumen* for breakfast, lunch, and dinner and coming up with crazy variations like salad-style, pasta-style, and udon-style *soumen* until the stinking sun goes down?! I'll send you whole boxes of the damn things if you want!!" she had flinched and given him the okay.

He didn't have much time until they met back up, so Kamijou's quick steps were lifeless as he headed back to the dormitory.

"Damn it. I should have considered the possibility of a trap at the supermarket when all those noodles were supercheap. This must be why nobody was buying them even for that price..."

And with perfect timing, after he'd bought way too much, his parents who lived outside Academy City had sent him a metric ton of dried noodles, saying, "We won a raffle at the store. You like *soumen*, too, right, Touma?" This part had been, as always, due to his rotten luck.

In any event, after getting back to his dorm, he saw Maika Tsuchimikado on her way out. This was generally a male dorm, but looking at the maid apprentice who came by just to clean her stepbrother's room and a certain hungry girl sprawled out in Kamijou's room, it seemed that public morals were becoming corrupted.

This girl, Maika, usually sat formally in seiza-style, with her legs tucked under her, atop an oil-drum-shaped automatic cleaning robot, but today she was walking normally. Her bangs were drawn back by the frilly headband unique to maids so most of her forehead could be seen. The outfit she wore was crazy—a dark-blue, long-sleeved maid uniform—but it must have been her school's designated uniform for the winter. She went to a home economics school.

Kamijou watched as she pattered up the passage. "Huh? What happened to your usual cleaning robot?"

"Heh-heh! I'm in such a good mood I can't wait for something so slow."

This girl's expressions were as hard to read as Aisa Himegami's, but happiness shined clear on her face like a lightbulb today. As Kamijou wondered what in the world could have happened, Maika put the back of her right hand to her cheek and laughed in a very unmaid-like, overbearing manner.

"Oh-ho-ho! It's this, this! My cuffs turned out great."

"Cuffs?"

"Yeah, you know, on my sleeves!" said Maika with a smile. "Maids aren't usually supposed to stand out. We can't have flashy hair or accessories or anything. So we show our individuality more surreptitiously in small things, like our cuffs and collars and stuff."

"Oh." He looked at her hands with renewed attention. Her sleeve fabric looked like it was folded back at her wrists. He couldn't tell what was different from usual. Was it like a girl being happy about getting her uniform for the first time and rolling up the waistband to make the skirt shorter?

Her face ecstatic, she rubbed her sleeve against her soft-looking cheek and sighed. "The gauntlet this morning really turned out great! I'm in a really good mood right now, so I'll listen to any worries you might have if you'd like."

"You will? Okay, then how would I get rid of a mountain of *soumen*?"

"Boil them first, then cut them up into small pieces and use them as the filling for a spring roll. It'll actually taste pretty much the same. It's an easy way to eat more of them at once!"

After answering, she pattered off somewhere at a trot. He could practically see the rays of happiness emitting from Maika just by watching her head off.

Kamijou stared after her for a few moments. "...Well, yeah. If you throw it into something with so much flavor, you're gonna lose the taste of whatever you threw in anyway."

Despite his brief, mumbled review of Maika's fairly offhanded reply, there was no point standing here, so he decided to enter his dorm.

After taking the rickety elevator to the seventh floor, he just had to go down the straight passage to arrive at his particular door in the line. Unlocking the door, he found the hungry girl, Index, inside, plopped down face-first in the middle of the floor. She was probably immobile from hunger again. Kamijou tossed his cheap bag to the side and said, "Noodles again today."

"Nooo!!" cried the pure-white-habit-wearing, silver-haired girl as she immediately bounded to her feet. Her green eyes glittered with deep dissatisfaction. "Why have you only been eating Japanese noodles this whole time?! Is this a ritual?! A kind of body-regulating sorcery that utilizes food culture?!"

Despite Index's whining and complaining, as soon as *soumen* actually made it to the table she'd have no hesitation scarfing it all down, so there was no big problem here. It was just beginning to get boring to eat all the time. Only temporarily, of course. She fundamentally loved the stuff, which is why she was stirred to such action. Kamijou nodded, then paused. "Love is tough."

"Touma?"

Index gave him a suspicious stare, but Kamijou didn't care.

There was a second freeloader in the room as well. The calico was basking in the sunlight by the door to the balcony. Until recently, he had always curled up in a place with a good draft, but now the seasons had changed. He had nothing to do with the *soumen*, so he could take it easy. Cat hair drifted about, too. Was his fur starting to adjust for winter? Kamijou was also pretty sure the cat was getting fatter, little by little.

As he reached for his street clothes so he could get changed in the bathroom, he said, "Anyway, Maika bestowed me with a secret technique earlier, and I'll be trying it immediately. Spring roll–style *soumen*! Let's go for it!"

"Maybe we should just have regular spring rolls?!" Index wailed, but before she could say any more, the intercom went off.

"Who could that be?"

Kamijou opened the door, and there stood Motoharu Tsuchimikado.

"Oh, you're in, nya. Kammy, sorry to ask, but I need your help with somethin', nya."

That put Kamijou on his guard. "H-help with what? You don't want me to go sink another world-class-sized magic fleet or anything, right?"

"Kammy…To think you can say things like that so smoothly now…Can I pity you?" After giving Kamijou a sympathetic look, Tsuchimikado continued, "No, not that. Maika made a little too much food, nya. She came here with a pot of something she said she slow cooked for ten hours, but I can't eat the whole thing. It would be a waste to throw it away, so if you want, you can have—"

"I'll eat it!!" shouted not Kamijou, but Index. She came rushing up behind him, ready to fling her landlord aside. There must have been a slight scent of food clinging to Tsuchimikado's clothes, because even the calico, who had been lounging, came trotting up to him.

Kamijou wanted to complain, but seeing Index's exceptional willingness to take up the offered meal, he decided to keep his mouth shut. The words *wise choice* came to mind.

Anyway, the party immediately moved next door, where Tsuchimikado lived.

The general layout of the room was exactly the same as Kamijou's, of course. But seeing training equipment everywhere, like the kind that could be found in a gym, changed the space's impression quite a bit. There were also two bookshelves leaning against the wall, packed with maid manga and things of that nature, a field for collectors. But Kamijou knew it was his duty as a friend to not mention that.

"Here it is," said Tsuchimikado, pointing out the table. Maika must have literally just dropped it off; a heavy-looking, silver stockpot, the kind a chef might use, had been placed on the table as is. Of course, a normal high school student wouldn't have a trivet they could use for something so giant, so the table was covered in old newspaper.

Tsuchimikado approached the pot and popped the lid open. Inside was an orange-colored stew.

"I think she used carrots for the base, but they completely broke up, nya. Then on top, she threw in ingredients like vegetables. It's one crazy stew, if you ask me."

"Aren't carrots kinda sweet?" That's what it seemed like, anyway, based on what he could smell. Maybe she hadn't used sugar and relied on the sweetness of the vegetables for flavor.

Whatever the case, they began ladling out the contents into large, shallow bowls. The potatoes and pork had been cut large. Quite a few different vegetables had been used; it was replete with health-conscious ingredients and considered nutrition that would normally be hard for a person to obtain during regular meals. Onions had been used as well, so they couldn't give any to the calico. Kamijou couldn't bring himself to meet the cat's eyes as it laid on the floor, seeming to say, *Come on, I want some, I want some, I want some!!*

Thus did lunchtime begin.

The meal was more extravagant than he'd expected, but he had to wonder about what he'd do with his *soumen*.

After thanking him for the food, Kamijou looked at Tsuchimikado, a spoon in one hand. "You're pretty generous. I mean, she says she's a maid in training, but isn't Maika's cooking level as good as some restaurants?"

"Nya~. That's why I offered. I can't just leave such valuable stuff uneaten, y'know? It's a bit hard for one guy to eat so much, nya."

"I see. I feel like you could have saved the stew, though."

Tsuchimikado suddenly froze.

This man generally did things like going out to eat, letting his stepsister make food for him, and basically acting like a student who can't cook for himself, which was unbecoming of someone living on his own. That's probably why he hadn't realized the possibility.

Touma Kamijou, one of those who could cook for himself, pushed on. "Also, if Maika made you this much food, doesn't that mean she won't be coming around for a while after this? Didn't she cook all this food so you'd have something healthy to save for later so you don't starve to death—?"

The calico was using its front legs to swat a boxlike thing around.

Looking at it, Kamijou could see the case was an airtight container for keeping food in. It was really big.

"..."

"..."

"..."

Kamijou, Index, and Tsuchimikado all looked around at one another.

They compared Maika Tsuchimikado's immense kindness with Motoharu Tsuchimikado's uselessness, then tried to imagine the sort of shadows that would be cast on the sunglasses-wearing boy's future if his long-haul stew was stolen from him.

They spent a few seconds in silence.

The calico meowed.

That was the starting signal. Kamijou and Index, at about the same time, began devouring the stew—*gobble, gobble, chomp, chomp, chomp, munch, munch, slurp, slurp, gobble!!*

Tsuchimikado paled and began rambling. "What?! Kammy, stop, stop!! I messed up I can't give any of this to you and hey listen to what I'm saying my sister's cooking belongs to me!!"

"Aha! Sorry, but you can't convince us by saying you'll hold on to it for us!! Besides, if you're gonna stop me, stop Index instead!! She's almost ready for seconds!!"

"Nyaaa?!" screamed Tsuchimikado.

Unfortunately, Index could no longer *be* stopped. Her spoon moved so quickly it looked like she'd gobble down the entire stew, pot and all.

How to put this—? It was another peaceful day.

INTERLUDE ONE

Lambeth Palace in London was originally a building designed to be the official residence of the English Puritan archbishop. Though its grounds were currently open as a sightseeing spot, unauthorized access to the inside of the building proper was forbidden, while all information was carefully sealed.

Put simply, nobody knew what the inside was like.

"Its existence is rife with mystery and intrigue" was the best anyone could guess from only viewing the historic-feeling exterior. If there was an English Puritan disciple conscious to some extent about status, influence, and the like, then they would know this palace was worthy of being called the end goal, somewhere the term *throne* could be used without it being an overstatement.

The building, with which normal people had no business and thus didn't consider its absolute privacy as suspicious, had a magical defense field stretched around it stronger than Buckingham Palace, where the queen resided. Those who needed VIP security were one thing, but even the gardeners and cleaners were all familiar with the highest level of close-combat anti-intruder magic, and everything—from the positions of pillars to the patterns on the wallpaper to the amount of light the western-style illumination gave off—had magical significance; it all functioned as *a singular trap*. Considering the palace itself was one large structure, the planners had designed it in an attempt to prevent any and all conventional intrusion attempts, as far-fetched a claim as that seemed. The clergymen and Iron Maidens sarcastically referred to it as the Nailed Bedroom.

At that moment, Lambeth Palace was veiled in midnight silence.

About nine hours separated Japan from England.

Despite less personnel present than during the day, the actual security level had shot up. And yet, this "invisible state of alert" went unnoticed. And inside...

...The archbishop Laura Stuart was in the bathroom.

"Hmm-hmm-hm-hmm-hmm-hmmm. ♪"

If the people who aspired to Lambeth Palace and imagined it as a high-class place were to look at that space, filled with light and echoing only with the sound of Laura's humming, they would have been petrified.

It was a bathroom, yes—but it was an enormous one, twenty meters square. However, it wasn't set up like a big communal bath. Instead, there were dozens of bathtubs packed tightly in the room.

Additionally, each tub had functions that absolutely reeked of the science side, whether they were electronic features, negative air ionization, jet stream massage, and so on.

It made sense. All the baths were symbols of the English Puritan rapport with Academy City and had been given to Laura as midyear and year-end gifts.

Right now, Laura was pulling her habit skirt up, sitting on the edge of the jet stream bathtub, dipping only her legs into the water.

She had a tub that was like a washbasin for her feet specifically, but she seemed to particularly like putting her feet in this jet stream.

Her golden locks, twice as long as she was tall, dripped with water. It had gotten to the point where it looked like a wet spiderweb, but she was planning to do her hair later, so it wasn't a problem. In any event, washing her feet came first.

Mmm...It just fills me with happiness! Now then, after my foot massage, I will use the sparky electric bath over there and warm my body...

As Laura Stuart continued to relieve the day's exhaustion…

…suddenly, without knocking, almost kicking down the door, Stiyl Magnus flew in.

"Archbishop!!"

Sporting red-dyed hair, a cigarette in his mouth, ten silver rings on his fingers, a bar code tattoo under his right eye and giving off a mixed smell of both perfume and nicotine was a mental, shouting priest.

Laura's entire body lurched in surprise. Though she was only washing her feet, she was in the middle of pulling up her skirt, exposing her bare legs. She frantically tried to push the hem back down, but the sudden motion caused her hips to slip off the tub's edge and tumble into it.

A crashing wave's splash echoed through the room.

Stiyl, holding a report in one hand, didn't stop to mind what had just happened. "Are the things written in this report true?! I *know* you didn't let your bonehead skills leak onto the paper again. The archbishop can change the world at a single word, so you need to… Stop making bubbles and complaining and answer me, please! You're the one who wrote this, are you not?!"

The bubbling wasn't actually coming from her trying to speak—the jet stream was suffocating her. But from Stiyl's point of view, she was just a woman acting merrily after falling in the tub with her legs up in an M shape and her panties on full display.

Laura pulled her face out of the stream with a *crsshh!!* "Wh-wha-what are you doing suddenly entering a lady's bathroom with your shoes on, Stiyl?! Y-you know you may be a clergyman and all— No, wait, it's precisely *because* thou art a clergyman that—"

"Shut. Up. And. Answer. Me!!"

"No, don't, Stiyl!! If you put your flame sword in the water, you'll boil my bath!!"

Laura half-stumbled, half-rolled her way out of the bathtub. A moment later, not only did it boil, but it also actually went up in a minor water vapor explosion. The archbishop had fallen to her knees on the sodden floor, mouth wide open and breathing heavily,

her superlong hair clinging to her like a cocoon and giving her the appearance of a monster.

Blood vessels stood out on Stiyl's temple. "It doesn't matter. Reread the contents of this report right now and explain the details to me. I'd like to get this job done and go to bed soon. Why must I look after this lonely woman...?"

But Laura wasn't listening to him. "Oh!! The water from before is making my habit cling to me and expose my impure, obscene body! This will not do! Look away, Stiyl! I have no intent whatsoever to display my undergarments to anyone!!"

"..." Another soft *crack*. Stiyl had crushed the cigarette filter in his mouth.

"W-wait, hold, Stiyl! If you stab me with a flame sword, I'll burn, I really will!!"

Laura ran away, and Stiyl chased her, flame sword in one hand.

It didn't look like he'd be getting any sleep tonight, either.

CHAPTER 2

What Kind of Punishment Game?
Pair_Contract.

1

Mikoto Misaka was in front of a concert hall.

They'd agreed to meet at that location.

"…Where are they?"

Around her, friends and couples met up with one another and then exited the hall. Being the only one stuck waiting was wearing on her.

Mikoto still wore her Tokiwadai Middle School uniform. She had her cheap schoolbag and her violin case with her. They'd get in the way while doing things, but bringing them back to her dorm would be a pain in its own right. Normally she could go in and out as she pleased, but if she was unlucky and got caught by an R.A., she could end up in an interrogation regarding the objective of her outing.

Instead, she'd come to the meeting place purposely without going back to the dorm first so she wouldn't be late. Of course, she had called up Kuroko Shirai, who was apparently nearby, to see if she could bring her things back for her.

"Why aren't either of them coming…?" muttered Mikoto absently.

She'd initially wanted to foist her things off on Shirai and spend the rest of her free time in a café, but the backbone of her plan hadn't arrived, so she'd been stuck standing around like this for a while.

She had put in so much effort to not be late, and yet Kamijou had no problems wasting her time. Why had she bothered trying to be so considerate? Mikoto sighed.

Still, she couldn't go back and drop her things off at her dorm now, since it was already past their agreed time. She might end up missing him on her way out.

She sighed again and slumped. "When I think about it, I don't know that idiot's phone number...Calling him would be too annoying anyway."

She was tired of standing now, too, so she squatted in place and put her bag and violin case on the ground. The bag's value was obviously low, but the case by itself was probably worth something as an antique. She didn't think about it much. A case just had to serve its purpose and nothing else.

As the young lady sat there with exhaustion emanating...

"There you are! You're Mikoto Misaka, right?"

A girl's bright voice called to her. Mikoto, hearing her name called, looked up in surprise.

She saw a middle school student standing there, smaller than her even. She had short black hair with a bunch of imitation flowers stuck in it, and she wore a sailor uniform. Mikoto thought she remembered the girl being part of the same Judgment branch as Kuroko Shirai. She usually hung around Shirai, though never directly talking to Mikoto.

"Oh...Kazari Uiharu, right?"

"Wow, you remembered!" Uiharu's eyes sparkled.

Her expression was the very definition of envy. But she didn't actually admire Mikoto the person, but rather Mikoto the upperclassman from the Tokiwadai Middle School she adored, a world of fancy and proper young ladies—so the way Uiharu's eyes sparkled was somewhat different from the way Shirai's did. This was purely a healthy level of respect.

Timidly, Uiharu said, "Um, I heard that Shirai was going to come here to carry your things, but..."

"Hmm?" Mikoto frowned.

Uiharu, staring at her schoolbag and violin case on the ground, said, "Um, well, Shirai is being forced to— Er, she's doing her best on a Judgment job right now. She says she'll be a little late. She really, really wants to come here, but since the timing didn't quite work out, she sent me here in her place!"

So that was it. Mikoto was about to nod, but then she froze.

She and Shirai were (to put it in a way that didn't evoke misunderstanding) familiar with each other, so Mikoto could ask her to do whatever. But Mikoto couldn't leave the job of carrying things to such a helpless, tender girl. Besides, Uiharu didn't even go to Tokiwadai. She wouldn't be able to get into the dorm, so she would have to hand her things over to someone else to bring them to her room.

If that someone happened to be an R.A., it would be really bad.

The great and powerful R.A., an *adult* lady, would probably greet Uiharu with a smile and gladly oblige her request, but when Mikoto returned to the dorm, there would be a demonic queen of rage waiting for her.

So Mikoto waved her hand casually in denial. "It's fine if Kuroko can't make it. I can just drop them off in a checkroom in some hotel nearby. And I could get a room and just use it for that, too."

"I see. I suppose you really can't just leave it in a coin locker." Uiharu was looking nervously at her violin case. Her body language was saying she had reservations handling something so valuable since she was only a regular person.

Mikoto waved her hand again. "No, no, no! I'm not doubting that you'll take good care of it, so you don't have to get all depressed!!"

"But…," Uiharu stammered. But she didn't continue and instead changed the topic. "Still, Tokiwadai Middle School really is amazing. It's not normal to use violins in school classes!"

"You think so? It's not really that difficult once you try it out." Mikoto noticed a subtle hint of envy in Uiharu's eyes as she stared at the violin. "Um, are you one of the types who worship our school?"

"N-no, no, not at all! I'm not like that!!" The way she lost her cool made it easy to understand. "A normal, average citizen like me would never be able to set foot in a place with so many proper young ladies!!"

"Well, I mean, if you have the talent, you can get as much financial assistance as you want. Our school appreciates what's inside more than what's outside. And I heard they flat out failed some royal girl once."

"I-if they cut off royalty, then that makes it even more of a super-hard zone to get into...Besides, I've never even held a violin before. It would be cool to be able to play it well, though..."

"I think it's like you're hating it without even trying..." Mikoto picked up the violin case from the ground. "Okay. Why not have a go?"

"Huh?! You're going to play for me?"

"No, you are."

"Bweehh?!" Uiharu looked at Mikoto in surprise, but the young lady from Tokiwadai quickly undid the case's clasps and took out the violin, which had an old, antique sheen to it, while also drawing out the bow needed to play the stringed instrument.

"Here, take it."

"Pfft?! P-please don't throw it!!"

She gingerly grasped the item she couldn't begin to imagine the value of. It didn't have to break—wouldn't its value go down just by getting sweat on it? Uiharu was frozen.

Mikoto stepped up next to her and started naming different parts of the violin. "Okay, try to do it like I said. You hold the violin with your left hand and hold that stick thing in your right. Place the butt of the violin between your jaw and your collarbone so it doesn't move. It's a cheap violin, so don't worry too much about being gentle with it."

So she said, but *cheap* meant *cheap* in a high-class lady sort of way. Uiharu wanted to shove the bomb in her hands back to Mikoto and run away, but if the violin cracked or something when she did, Uiharu was pretty sure it'd stick with her the rest of her life. She couldn't do something so bold.

Mikoto watched Uiharu, who had frozen up and wasn't even moving a finger, giving the girl a questioning stare. "Sorry, sorry. I guess it's hard to understand just from me telling you."

"Y-yes, it is."

"Then I'll teach you with my hands. You do it like this."

"*Wehh?!*" cried Uiharu. Mikoto had gently put her arms around Uiharu's back and taken the violin. It was like a mother gently teaching her young child how to play.

Uiharu seized up even more intensely at her sudden proximity, but Mikoto, pressed up against her back, didn't mind at all. Whether by coincidence or not, Uiharu could feel Mikoto's breath on her ear as she began her lecture.

"It's important to hold down the strings with your left fingers, but first comes learning to use the bow. It might look hard, but you just have to remember what angles produce which sounds and it's easy."

Mikoto's graceful hands, which had joined Uiharu's from above, began to move. The result was a single drawn-out, weak-sounding note, the kind you might hear when tuning an instrument.

Uiharu, who happened to be red-faced and dizzy-eyed, hadn't heard much of Mikoto's instructions, but Mikoto, in her own way, was completely unaware of that. As long as it wasn't someone like Shirai, Mikoto was generally very kind to girls.

"You play the violin differently depending on how you use your left hand. Pizzicato, glissando, flagioletto. There's a bunch, but none of them are very hard, so we'll try each of them. Don't even sweat it. You'll get used to it in no time. You'll be fine."

The warmth particular to a human's skin traveled to Uiharu's back; she felt a sweet breath at her ears and the fingers of two hands wrapped gently around her own… *Th-this must be the young lady hierarchy thing Shirai is so absorbed with!!*

Finally, Mikoto realized Uiharu had grown completely stiff. In an attempt to soothe the young girl's nerves, she said, "It's all right. This is a big hall, and there are no restrictions on giving performances. You don't have to worry about people paying attention to you if you're playing an instrument."

"N-no, that's not…Wait, a performance?! Hyaa, all of a sudden there's a whole crowd here, and I feel like the center of attention…"

Uiharu paused midway through her surprised cry.

*　　*　　*

Because…

In that mass, she'd spotted Kuroko Shirai, who wore a fierce expression on her face.

"Gyaaaaaaaaaaaaaaaahhh!!" Uiharu's shoulders gave a jolt.

Unnatural strength entered her arms, causing a grating *greeee* sound to come out of the violin.

As Shirai watched, she unleashed all her mental energy toward her colleague who stood in the center of the congregation.

"…Ah, I see how it is. I knew her praiseworthy offer to help me carry things was unusual, and here we are. I see she had an ulterior motive, and I can never drop my guard because this is what happens and not even I've gotten her to look at me with such sweet, sweet eyes—Big Sister…!"

Judging by her face, it seemed she was about to trip over a television cord.

Kazari Uiharu broke out into a cold, profuse sweat, but Mikoto Misaka, as always, didn't notice.

"Is something wrong?"

"N-no, nothing at all!!"

"Is someone giving you suspicious looks?"

"You shouldn't say that!!"

Uiharu spoke with her eyes almost filled with tears, but Mikoto didn't give a thought to Shirai's presence the entire time.

2

Their meeting time was one PM.

"It's already one thirty! What the heck happened?!" echoed the shout of Mikoto Misaka, who stood all by herself in front of the concert hall, which was a fairly prominent location in the Seventh School District.

Kamijou put his hands together and bowed in a gesture of apology as he dashed over to her. "Hey, I'm really sorry!!"

He'd actually been late because their food problems with Motoharu Tsuchimikado had evolved into a minor fistfight, but Kamijou knew it would be better for him not to make any lame excuses and just apologize.

Mikoto, for her part, folded her arms while tapping her foot on the ground and letting bluish-white sparks crackle and spark from her bangs. "I'm the one who won the bet for the punishment game, so why am I being made subject to your circumstances? Do you have any idea what it feels like to be embarrassed and standing by myself doing nothing for a whole hour? Weird, stupid boys came up trying to talk to me while I was waiting, and it was a huge pain in the butt to drive them all away with lightning lances, you know."

"Okay, okay! I'm really sorry!" Kamijou said, attempting to continue their exchange by saying nothing of substance whatsoever, before suddenly noticing something odd in what Mikoto said. "Wait, what? The meeting time was at one, right?"

"...Don't tell me you even ignored that part."

"No, not that. If you've been waiting here for an hour, then you got here a half hour early, right? That's...well, sorry about that."

Mikoto's shoulders gave a jerk, and her eyes widened. She unfolded her arms and started waving her hands in front of her. "No...Y-you're an idiot. That's just a manner of speaking. It's not like I've been here exactly sixty minutes now or anything. Wh-why do I have to wait for you when I'm the one who won the bet, anyway? I wish you'd wipe that dumb smirk off your face. It looks like you're imagining something strange."

"You know...," said Kamijou without thinking, looking straight at the middle school girl's face as she wavered. "...You enjoy watching me suffer through this punishment game *that much*? I mean, I thought this already, but you're actually pretty underhanded, aren't—?"

Before he could finish, a lance of lightning leaped from Mikoto's bangs.

Kamijou immediately swung his hand up to block the attack. *Zztchhh!!* From what he could tell by the intense bursting noise, the voltage was in the hundred million range.

In his right hand was a power called Imagine Breaker, which had a nullifying effect on any strange powers, whether magical or supernatural, with a single touch.

It was still scary.

As he trembled, he said this: "...I was right?"

Another lightning lance shot at him.

Everyone gathered in front of the concert hall shouted, "Whoa!!" at the huge *ka-bang!!* and ran away. Kamijou, who just barely managed to stop it in time again, was a little teary-eyed.

"What is it?! Miss Misaka, I don't know which words are the ones you want to hear!!"

"It doesn't matter. Just come on," said Mikoto, the corners of her lips twitching, her head slowly tilting. In a low voice, she continued, "...You're the one who lost, so quit fighting against the winner, you stupid piece of trash."

"This proper Tokiwadai lady is acting a little weird right now!!" cried Kamijou, but Mikoto, extremely unhappy for some reason, didn't give him much of a reaction.

He scratched his head. The situation was not going in a good direction. "Anyway, Misaka, what exactly should I do for the punishment game? You said 'Come on,' so are we going somewhere else?"

The moment she heard that...

Mikoto grunted, looking somewhat surprised.

She looked at him.

Kamijou was fed up. "...Don't tell me you didn't think of anything..."

"I—I'm thinking right now! Um, well, er, yeah! You're gonna pay me back for all the effort I put in to win the Daihasei Festival!!"

"So, you weren't thinking anything specific."

"Would you just listen?!"

"You're the one who suggested this, so you're the one who has to think of a plan. I mean, you knew from the start that I wouldn't be the one making plans, right? I'm the one who lost. Sheesh, what an idiot."

"..." Mikoto fell silent for a moment. Then she looked at Kamijou again.

"Um, Misaka...*Urgh?!*"

Kamijou, about to talk to the girl who wouldn't say anything, then unconsciously took a step back.

The reason was simple.

There was a glazed look in the proper young lady's eyes.

Kamijou had a really bad feeling about this.

"You'll do whatever I say for the punishment game, right?"

"Well, er...! By 'anything,' it's anything I'm actually able to do, so...!!"

"*Whatever I say?*"

"..."

"Come with me."

"Where?!" Kamijou shouted, but Mikoto grabbed his hand with a *slap!!* and wouldn't let go. As she dragged him away, the concert hall began to grow distant behind them.

The girl spoke again. "I told you, just shut up and come with me! That's your first punishment!!"

"The first one?! There's more than one?!"

Touma Kamijou grew pale for some reason, and Mikoto Misaka's face reddened in anger.

They walked down the street, hands firmly connected, but whether fortunate or unfortunate, neither of them noticed.

3

Accelerator was looking up at an apartment complex built for faculty.

Academy City's residences were generally nothing but student dorms. Apartments like these were not something a student had much to do with.

From the building's exterior, it didn't look much different from a student dorm or any other apartment complex, but there were tiny differences in terms of service, and everything added up to give it individuality.

No matter how they were presented, student dorms were buildings meant to supervise children. Under the pretext of security, the dorms' surveillance cameras were positioned without hold back in the slightest, which was characteristic of school-provided lodgings. In comparison, this apartment had a certain degree of consideration for the residents' privacy.

"What floor?" asked Accelerator.

Aiho Yomikawa, who had guided them here, answered with a smile, "Thirteen. When the power goes out, I have to use the stairs. It's a huge pain."

"Wow!" breathed Last Order as she looked up at the tall building. She looked like she was trying to find the thirteenth floor, but now she was shaking her head, having accidentally looked directly at the sun.

Kikyou Yoshikawa supported the small girl's shoulders from behind to keep her upright. "Well, compared to the first or second floor, I'd think there would be fewer chances to raid it."

"…If they blew up the whole building, the people on the top floors would have way more casualties." Nothing that major had happened to Accelerator while he lived in his dorm, but that didn't mean for sure it would never happen.

As Yomikawa removed a laminated card, probably to use on the entrance's auto-locking mechanism, she said, "Anyway. It's a little late for lunch, but you still need to eat, so let's get ourselves up there, 'kay?"

At first glance, the complex's entrance looked like a normal, automatically opened glass door, but it showed signs of being blast-proof. The lock that only needed a card swipe also appeared to actually be reading additional data, such as fingerprints from the fingers holding the card and patterns in bioelectric signals.

It was what you would perhaps call a high-class apartment building. Accelerator glanced at Yomikawa suspiciously. "And here I thought public workers' salaries were going down."

"You can still get by on a pretty low salary. Plus, this place is a *facility*, or rather a field test for architectural design, so some of the rent is paid by the universities. In exchange, they switch up security methods on us every once in a while.

"Plus," she added, "Anti-Skill officers are generally volunteers, so we don't get paid for those services. But people here and there do us surprising favors, like meat at the supermarket being cheaper for us."

"...Treating apartment rent the same as sales at the store?"

All told, the group of four—Accelerator, Last Order, Yomikawa, and Yoshikawa—entered the complex. As an aside, Komoe had other errands to attend to, so she wasn't here right now.

They took a low-vibration elevator that imparted no floating feeling—probably another trial product—to the thirteenth floor. Yomikawa's room was the door right outside when they stepped out.

"Come on in," said Yomikawa, opening the front door, revealing a large apartment with a living room, dining room, kitchen, and four other rooms. It was, by all accounts, made for a family and big enough for one to spend their entire life paying it off. Although the universities exempted her from a certain portion of the cost since she was helping with experiments, could a public worker's low salary really "get by"?

The living room had a floor that was polished to a shine and, unlike the stereotypical mess expected when hearing one person lived here alone, was neatly organized. Bottles of alcohol and glasses decorated the shelving, while magazines and newspapers had their own racks. Remote controls for the TV, the air conditioner, the stereo, and the video recorder were all lined up on a table corner. Each of the sofa cushions were precisely placed in their proper positions.

Last Order's eyes went wide. "Amazing, I don't think there's a single speck of dust in here, says Misaka says Misaka with praise as she leaps onto the couch."

In contrast to Last Order's cheerful voice as she sank into the couch, Yoshikawa sighed. "...They made you file another written apology at your job, didn't they?"

Yomikawa gulped, her tracksuit-clad body wavering. "Ah, ah-ha-ha. What're ya talkin' about?"

"What do you mean? asks Misaka asks Misaka, lying around confused."

"I'm just saying she's always had a habit of cleaning her place whenever problems crop up. She doesn't think about the future when she's doing it, either, so later on she has trouble finding things like her room key. I want you to be careful, all right?"

"Is that any way to talk to the person doing you a favor by helping you look for your next job?"

Accelerator noted to himself that Yomikawa and Yoshikawa got a lot more childish in their word choice and behavior when they talked to each other. Or maybe it showed how long they'd been friends. If Yoshikawa was the caring class president type, Yomikawa was the consistently late problem child.

Yoshikawa glanced toward the kitchen, which connected to the living room. "If you haven't grown out of that habit yet, then you must still have the same kitchen manners."

"Hey, heeey! I'll admit I have bad habits when keeping things clean, but it's annoying when you mention that! Kikyou, you've gobbled down my cooking without a second thought, haven't you?"

"Only when I don't know how you made it."

Accelerator and Last Order exchanged confused glances. Yomikawa led Yoshikawa into the kitchen, claiming she was "getting better every day, and I'll show you!" They followed.

Yomikawa's kitchen was filled with all sorts of cooking equipment, under the pretext of "assisting in experiments." It was a conglomeration of super high-tech stuff, from a steam microwave that used water vapor to things like an AI-controlled high-frequency fully automatic dishwasher.

She didn't seem to use any much, though.

What stood out a lot more than those appliances, which had an air of disuse that screamed they were just abandoned like that all the time, were the four or five electric rice cookers laid out. Given the steam wisping from them, they all seemed to be on.

Accelerator gave her an exasperated look. "...One for each of us? Is this some kind of joke? Do you have a fetish for white rice?"

"No, no, that's not it!" Yomikawa pointed to each of the rice cookers in turn. "You know, rice cookers can do anything—cook rice, boil things, steam things, and bake things...That one's baking bread, that one's cooking stew, and that one's steaming whitefish."

"..." Accelerator thought he knew what Yoshikawa was trying to say now.

Yoshikawa, who already knew about all this, sighed at how little had changed and said, "Lazy bum."

"I'd like it if you stopped with the brief commentary like I'm a strange animal. Is it really that bad? All I have to do is set them up, press one button, and they'll cook things for me. They don't use gas, either, so I can feel free to take a nap while it's happening with no problem at all. They're amazing, really..."

"You used to say you could make *okonomiyaki* out of whatever leftovers you had as long as you had flour, and you bought a giant hot plate for it. And you would complain that as long as you had a pressure cooker, you'd be set for cooking for the rest of your life and didn't need anything else...You go too far with everything. You're so extreme that if you split the distance there'd be an antimatter reaction."

"I'm getting all the flavor, nutrition, and satisfaction I need, so what's the problem? Stockpots, frying pans...It's a pain to get all those things together. Wouldn't you want a miracle tool that could do everything?"

Yoshikawa sighed. "For once in your life you should feel how enjoyable it is to put actual effort into cooking," she admonished, but in the same way, her field of specialty was genetics. On further consideration, she felt her comment held less weight, considering what she had made was twenty thousand cloned humans.

4

After leaving her violin at a coat check, Mikoto dragged Kamijou into the underground mall.

It had suffered considerable damage thanks to the sorcerer Sherry Cromwell and the golem she controlled, Ellis. They had arrived from England on September 1, but no traces of the destruction could be seen any longer. The smashed floors and support beams had been repaired, and things like café windows had been replaced with new ones. Without getting up close to look, it was probably impossible to see the difference.

The construction had proceeded at such a fever pitch because the Daihasei Festival had been fast approaching. Half the reason for the festival was propaganda meant to improve Academy City's image, so leaving the city in tatters was out of the question. (Though it had been wrecked quite a bit the day of as well.)

Though it was underground, it didn't feel dark; the floors and walls had been polished to a sparkle, illuminated by fluorescent lighting and LED bulbs, bundles of light-emitting diodes, as if by a summer sun. Hallway-facing shops, like cafés and western clothing stores, made abundant use of glass, granting them a sense of openness that exceeded their actual size.

Kamijou looked around and said, "Huh, looks like they turned down the air-conditioning."

"They'll probably switch to heating in another two weeks," said Mikoto as she plodded ahead. "Oh, there it is! Over here." She pointed to a store with a slender finger.

The mall fully utilized the fact that it was underground and was equipped with loud entertainment facilities such as arcades, karaoke boxes, and music venues. That's why Kamijou was thinking she'd make him try to beat a superhard arcade game on a single credit or else have to grovel before her...But his prediction was way off.

It was a cell phone service store.

It was only about half the size of a convenience store. Through its big glass windows a line of counters and chairs could be seen, plus a catalog of cheap devices filling a magazine rack—that was all. In front of the entrance was a long, vertical *banner* for advertising, dividing big manufacturers' products from ones only made in Academy City.

Academy City was said to be two or three decades ahead of the rest of the world in science and technology. Devices from both outside and inside had their own advantages and disadvantages, but some students worried about their decision for over a week for reasons like not knowing which would have access to service first in emergencies.

As Mikoto walked toward the service store, she asked, "Have you heard of the Handy Antenna Service?"

"Huh? It's that, uh, service that makes your personal cell phone like an antenna station, right? So you can call people without having antenna stations nearby?"

Basically, it would make everyone walking through the city streets with a cell phone into a relay antenna. For example, even if Kamijou didn't have an antenna station nearby, it would go through person one, then person two, and person three, through various relay antennas, to eventually call person X provided that person had a normal antenna station close to them. In practical terms, it created a network-like communication route through multiple other devices, which meant disconnections were rare. Apparently, it had originally been developed to maintain emergency aerial networks by attaching fixed antennas to a few airships, then sending them up in the air—all in case the relay stations on the ground had been wiped out in a disastrous earthquake. Because of that, he'd heard, people didn't seem to care too much about sound quality.

On the plus side, he'd also heard that the universities would subsidize it all as a test, so the service fees were supposedly way cheaper.

"I was thinking of signing up for it."

"Yeah? It seems like a really esoteric system to me. If everyone using it didn't have their cell phones on constantly, you couldn't hope for any of that relay antenna stuff to work. Wouldn't your battery drain a lot more quickly that way? And besides, if not many people have signed up for the service, there isn't much point in—"

"That's why I'm signing up for it, dummy—to spread it around more. And apparently, if we sign up for a pair contract, the fees for other services go down, not just the Handy Antenna Service."

"A pair contract…? You mean that thing where two people sign up and don't have to pay to talk to each other or for packet fees and stuff?"

"Yeah, that. On top of that, if you sign up for a pair contract with the Handy Antenna Service, you get a Croaker cell phone strap from Lovely Mitten. It's their frog mascot."

"…Oi."

"Right on the spot. So, you're signing up with me."

"All you wanted was the cell phone strap?! If you want me to change devices, then that's not gonna happen! I still plan on using my old, beat-up cell phone for another six months at least!!" Then Kamijou pointed at the blazer-clad Mikoto's schoolbag. He stared at a green frog mascot character hanging from it. "Besides, you already have a frog!"

"Don't lump together Croaker with this one!!" Mikoto shouted angrily. "Croaker is the older man living next to this guy, and he's bad with vehicles and starts croaking a lot when he's in them, which is why they call him Croaker! Maybe you're actually a really old man! I mean, you couldn't even tell such a simple difference!!"

"…They made his character an old guy? And they call themselves *lovely*?" muttered Kamijou, disheartened.

Mikoto, though, just continued to look at him scornfully as though he were an elderly person who couldn't keep up with the times. "Hmph. You don't need to worry about changing devices. I hear you don't have to switch them anyway for Handy Antenna. You just put an expansion chip in your phone and you're good to go. And whatever service you have, they'll deal with the pair contract, too, so I don't think you have to switch devices. You shouldn't have to mess with your phone at all."

"What? Wait, so all I have to do is write my phone number and address on the form?"

"Well, yeah, but..." Mikoto absently fingered the small frog attached to her schoolbag. "I mean, we go together to the store, have to sign a lot of forms, and probably wait for hours. I have to get someone considerate to help me out or it'll be hard to convince them. Anyway, it's not like it'll actually take half a day, so bear with it for a little bit."

"Hmm." Kamijou thought about it, glancing at the store's *banner*. Did she bring him here because she had to be paired with a boy? That meant...

"? What's wrong?"

"No, well, I don't mind signing up with you, but...This pair contract thing. Isn't it normally meant for couples? It says here it has to be one man and one woman."

"...?!" Mikoto's shoulders gave a jerk. Her hand squeezed the frog mascot on her bag. "N-no, no, don't be stupid, what the heck are you talking about, you idiot?! I-it only says it has to be a girl and a boy, not that they have to be a couple or anything, so I mean, married people could do it, too, you know!!"

"Hello? Miss Misaka, that's a little heavier than your average couple."

All he wanted to do was make a calm rejoinder, but a moment later, a lightning lance flew at him. He hastily repelled the strike from Mikoto's bangs with his right hand. "What the heck is up with you lately?!"

"Y-you're the one not making any sense here! Could we just get this over with already?!"

"What? We're actually doing this?!"

"Look, it's your punishment game, so stop complaining and come with me!"

Mikoto grabbed Kamijou's arm and dragged him inside the service store.

Compared to the underground mall's passages, the air-conditioning inside the store was a little more *polite*. Kamijou knew that was a strange way of describing it, but they had it at just the right level—like they calculated all the ventilation routes or something, so even though he didn't feel the chill on his skin, his sweat vanished.

The female employee sitting in front of one of the counters broke into a smile at seeing them come in, though Kamijou was being dragged and Mikoto was the one pulling him along, but she didn't forget what it said in the manual about interacting with customers.

After a brief exchange in which Mikoto talked about wanting to sign up for a pair contract with the idiot accompanying her and wondering aloud whether they still had Croaker straps, the employee laid out many documents on the counter before them.

"We will need a photograph to complete the forms. Do you happen to have one on your person?"

"Huh?" grunted Mikoto, her eyes widening, then asked, "Will it need to be from a photo ID box? Also, is there a certain number of pictures or a specific size we need?"

"No, not at all. The rules aren't that strict." The employee smiled. "Since this is a pair contract, all we need is for you to prove that you two are the pair who signed up for it. As long as you're both in the shot together, you can even use your cell phone camera. I'll get a picture frame battery charger for your phone so you can use that. It's made to fit any of the four major providers, so you needn't worry about the model number."

Mikoto almost sputtered. "...B-both of us in the shot?"

"Oh, do you not take pictures of yourselves very often? Then why not use this chance to? You'll just need to give me a photograph twenty minutes before the sign-up process is done, so please, use the time you'd be waiting to take a picture."

And so, after jotting various details on the forms with a ballpoint pen, Kamijou and Mikoto left the service store for the time being to embark on the aforementioned picture taking.

Kamijou took out his cell phone, which was quite hardy considering he'd damaged it in battles with sorcerers and dropped it into the Adriatic Sea. "Finding a photo ID booth would be a pain, so let's just use a cell phone camera and get this over with. You don't have any other digital cameras or anything, right, Misaka?"

"Huh? Oh yeah, well, I left my phone with the lady at the counter, so..."

Mikoto sounded somehow absentminded, but Kamijou didn't notice. He looked at his phone screen and pressed a couple buttons with his thumb, switching it into camera mode, then reached out to get the phone as far away from them as he could. Still looking at the screen, he said, "Okay, I'm taking it... Wait."

"Wh-what?" asked Mikoto, confused.

Kamijou made a face. He hadn't noticed, but Mikoto was pretty far away from him. She looked like she was waiting for him to switch into panorama mode and take the picture already because she was getting impatient.

She looked ready to run away. Kamijou's shoulders drooped. "...You're the one who suggested this. I'm just saying."

"I...I know that!!" cried Mikoto, her face getting a little red as she waved her hands in the air before her along with her schoolbag. It didn't look too friendly to Kamijou.

After Mikoto vacillated on whether to get closer to him or farther away, she finally groaned in resignation. "I'm coming for you, Croaker!!"

In one breath, she drew right up to Kamijou so their shoulders were touching, then bent her head a little to put it on his shoulder. Their faces were both right in the middle of the cell phone screen.

Meanwhile, Kamijou had begun to think she didn't need to get *this* close to him and stiffened a little at the scent of her hair.

"O-okay, I'm taking it."

"Got it! I'm ready!!"

Pchee!! sounded the camera shutter, a noise that sounded purposely electronic.

Kamijou brought his cell phone back toward him and checked the picture he'd just taken.

...

"You're grimacing, Misaka."

"Why are you looking away like you're trying to get away from me?"

They exchanged glances.

"I don't think this is a good pair picture."

"L-let's try taking another one."

Pchee!! came the electronic sound again.

They peered at the cell phone screen.

"Why is your face so stiff again, Misaka?!"

"And why do you look like you're trying to put more distance between us?!"

Grr!! They glared at each other, their faces so close their foreheads almost bumped. They wouldn't get anywhere at this rate. In the worst-case scenario, they would need to apologize for not having a picture and cancel the sign-up process, and all their work thus far would be for nothing. Troubling for them but also a major hassle for the employee.

Kamijou gave up. "Anyway, we just have to make it look like we're a couple for this, right?! Misaka, come here! This is what I'm gonna do!!"

"Huh? What? Kyaa!!"

He forcefully looped an arm around her slender shoulders as her face immediately went bright red. Kamijou didn't notice; he was already in desperation mode.

"Smile, Misaka! I don't want to have to take one like this again! It doesn't matter what it is as long as we can put it on the form! There's a clear reason, so there's no problem doing this!!"

"Huh? W-well, I guess you're right, ah-ha-ha! We're just taking a picture that *looks* like that, right? Yeah, that's right. Just taking a picture! Okay, let's do this!!"

Slightly miffed by the bit about "clear reason," Mikoto forced herself to be happy, not wanting her desperation—or rather, her blush—to be noticed. To match Kamijou's closeness, she put her arm around his and drew in closer. A few passersby saw the two of them...no, Mikoto and some random boy. Those people stared at them with a little bit of envy. But the pair was too wound up to notice.

Kamijou brought his phone out in front of them. "I'm taking it!"

"Yes!!"

Before the shameless electronic *pchee!!* could go off...

...Kuroko Shirai suddenly appeared with teleportation and delivered a drop kick to the back of Touma Kamijou's head.

With a thunderous *craaack*, the cell phone flew from Kamijou's hands as his body slammed forward, the phone's shutter going off a moment later.

Despite his intention for the picture to be a cute shot of a couple, Kamijou saw the phone, now resting on the ground, display instead a flawless shot of his blurry head, a surprised Mikoto, and Shirai's underwear.

Kamijou had tumbled down to the floor face-first. "Wh-what the hell?!"

"I...I take my eyes off you for five minutes, and what do you do...?" Kuroko Shirai landed from her drop kick right next to Mikoto. It seemed like she was implying that was her spot, not his. "First, Uiharu makes me do grunt work for Judgment after a half day's worth of classes, then when that's finally finished and I go see Big Sister, Uiharu was waiting for me with a violin attack, and *then* they made me do an extra job where I put in so much effort...Good grief, I see it was a mistake to underestimate you as an upstart slave. Big Sister, you've certainly been having your fill..."

"I...Don't read anything into this, Kuroko!" Mikoto's hands flailed around in an expression of denial. "I wasn't doing this because I wanted to! I mean it! I just wanted the Croaker strap, so I asked him to sign up for a pair contract with me, and they told us we had to take a photo for it!!"

A listener could take that as her convincing herself of the fact rather than defending herself to Shirai. Whatever the case, there was no point kicking Kamijou or asking him for anything.

Well, this was how punishment games usually went.

Shirai couldn't completely conceal her shock at what Mikoto said.

"But! But you needn't beg a gentleman like *him* for help! If you'd asked me to pair with you, Big Sister, there wouldn't have been any issue! Now, I'll take a picture, let's get this over with quickly, we're about to make a memory that will last a lifetime!!"

Mikoto gave a slight grimace to Shirai, who had instantaneously boiled over, but Kamijou abruptly looked back up.

"Huh? If that's fine, then can I go home now?"

"I told you, the couple needs to be a boy and a girl!!"

The crude question resulted in Mikoto firing a powerful spear of lightning at him.

5

On the sofa he'd been sleeping on, Accelerator opened his eyes slightly.

He sucked his teeth. "…Must've fallen asleep."

Checking the clock, he saw it had only been about fifteen minutes.

They'd left the TV on. The noise it was making had probably woken him up. Lately he'd been waking up without much reason, whether he was just sleeping more lightly or because of sudden stimulus.

In the wide, empty living room, Accelerator shook his head a little. *I let my guard down. Idiot, idiot.* His own resentful voice seeped into his mind.

Accelerator had always slept whenever he wanted. Alarm clocks ringing next to his ears, stupid kids raising hell, or bombs exploding on top of him—no matter what, he would continue to sleep peacefully through it all.

That was thanks to his ability, which could change any vectors at will. Normally he'd always be "reflecting" everything except the bare minimum oxygen and gravity he needed.

In that state, Accelerator could take a direct hit from a nuclear bomb and emerge unscathed.

That was why Accelerator, who had innumerable enemies, never hesitated to fall asleep—which could be called his most defenseless state—before now.

Unfortunately, that was back when his ability was perfect.

Accelerator put a hand to his neck.

Around it was a blackish choker…or what looked like one, except it had electrodes attached to the inside. It was a device that linked to the brains of a little less than ten thousand Sisters scattered throughout the world, letting him borrow their immense parallel calculation functions.

Accelerator had suffered brain damage on August 31.

This device and the calculation assistance it offered him were the only things letting him live a normal life now. In normal mode, he could retain his ability to walk, speak, and count for forty-eight hours, but normal in this case was esper mode—when he activated all his vector control abilities, he would have to do a ton of calculations in the span of an instant, so the battery would go dead in fifteen minutes. The item came with quite a few limitations.

This all meant that, practically speaking, he could only be safe for fifteen minutes at a time.

Beyond those fifteen minutes, he was a weakling who couldn't even walk properly unless he charged the battery once every forty-eight hours.

Now that he was in such a situation, he could no longer languish in indolence and laziness, sheltered behind his abilities.

"…"

Accelerator, his eyes suspicious, glanced at the huge flat-screen TV.

A one o'clock talk show was displayed on a cable channel boasting stupidly high contract pricing. Given the video recorder currently active underneath the TV, he guessed that Yomikawa, the owner, was a fan of the celebrity appearing on the show today or something.

"Mr. Hajime Hitotsui, tell us a little about the movie you starred in recently. Japanese people having a lead role in overseas productions is fairly rare, isn't it? Can you tell us about what that felt like?"

The MC and the guest were facing each other across a small table.

As Accelerator stared at the screen, his hand moved to the switch on the side of the electrode choker…

…and cut the power.

*   *   *

"Well. The most unique directive on the side of the plot was to use it to act appropriately as a Japanese. Maybe he didn't have even and the other people extremely appropriately understood it as a Japanese person today?"

The words came out garbled.

The guest had actually said this: "Well, the most unique instruction the director gave me was simply to act like a Japanese person would. I mean, even *we* don't really know what that means these days, do we?" However, Accelerator's brain couldn't parse the conversation's contents anymore.

He started to lose his balance.

Almost before he realized he was falling, his body was back down on the sofa. The digital numbers on the video recorder—he couldn't understand what they meant. The gears in his mind had disconnected. It was like he was looking at a problem on a standardized test after someone forced him to stay awake with no rest for a hundred hours.

*Urgh…*Accelerator put his hand to his neck.

His body felt like it was wobbling all over the place, and it took several seconds for him just to flip the small switch. After hitting the choker a few times and failing, the middle of his thumb eventually found it.

There was a soft *click*.

It changed into normal mode, returning Accelerator at last to the usual world.

"I had to use native American English for actually speaking, so he told me to display what being Japanese means through only my actions, behavior, and attitude. It made me think a lot about it."

In his sideways perspective of the world, what was undeniably the celebrity's bragging session continued.

Once they'd called Accelerator the strongest esper in Academy City. Now he was reduced to this.

If he didn't borrow the proxy calculations of Last Order and the rest of the Sisters, he wouldn't be able to have a normal conversation, walk, or even count to ten, much less use his ability. The electrode choker on his neck was essential for that task, and the battery could hold out for forty-eight hours max.

And if the power ran out or he went underground or somewhere that otherwise obstructed the electric signals, he wouldn't be able to use it.

Just the choker's normal mode had brought him to this.

It had to process much more information in ability usage mode, and he'd only be able to use it in that state for a little under fifteen minutes. Its primary use was first and foremost as a medical device, not something that could stand up to the military-level usage required in the environment of esper combat. The battery was also something the frog-faced doctor had made especially for this—he couldn't change it, swap it with a store-bought battery or anything. He also couldn't get a whole bunch of batteries together and chain them in and out to increase the usage time.

Fifteen minutes was, in all truth, his time limit.

At least he wouldn't need to use his crutch anymore in ability mode.

It's such a pain to have to remember every goddamn one of those rules. What am I, freakin' Cinderella? Supreme but with a time limit? That's not even funny.

" . . . "

Guess I'll take a shower, thought Accelerator, rising from the sofa.

He needed a change in pace.

Last Order, utterly without caution 24-7, was one thing. Yomikawa and Yoshikawa were just too soft. Why was everyone he met putting so much trust in the "strongest" esper in the city? Who said he'd be able to meet any of those expectations? Yomikawa and Yoshikawa didn't understand the terror. Sure, he was accustomed to destroying things, but he wasn't used to protecting others at all. And if he did strike for a defensive purpose, it was easy to imagine the danger developing into a catastrophe that engulfed everything nearby.

Huh. Nobody's in the room. Did those idiots go shopping or something? thought Accelerator idly as he opened the door to the changing room.

And there...

...was Last Order, completely naked, her soggy brown hair being dried off with a towel...

...by Yomikawa and Yoshikawa on either side of her.

Last Order was the first to react with a sudden jerk. "Wh-why do you keep showing up out of the blue like that?! says Misaka says Misaka, reaching for her towel but not reaching it and stuff!!"

Accelerator ignored the noise coming from Last Order and looked at Yomikawa and Yoshikawa, who were standing there blankly.

"...Why the hell didn't you lock the door?"

"Er, sorry about that, 'kay? Been living on my own and everything, so I totally forgot that was a thing. Sowwy, sowwy."

"Aiho, would you please just cover yourself already?" asked Yoshikawa with a sigh and handed a towel to her counterpart—she'd already wrapped herself in one. Yomikawa, looking annoyed, covered herself with it. Even so, her thighs were more exposed than if she'd been wearing a miniskirt, and he could see her silhouette pretty clearly, given that she hadn't dried herself off yet.

...What the hell is this?

This wasn't what Accelerator's life was like. If there were a person who ran into women changing or whatever whenever he opened a door, he'd be laughing his ass off right now.

Last Order realized there weren't enough towels for her, panicked, and hid herself behind Yoshikawa, eyes watering. "...Why are you two simply handing towels to each other like you're tired and without making a fuss? asks Misaka asks Misaka bluntly."

"Huh?" Yomikawa looked at Last Order dubiously. "Well, I mean...He's a kid, and we're adults, 'kay?"

"Not caring about it whatsoever is more the hallmark of a middle-aged lady than just an adult, I think, says Misaka...*Ow, ow, ow, ow!!* Stop ·pressing on Misaka's head like that! insists Misaka insists Misaka with resolution and stuff!!"

As Yoshikawa continued her attack on the crown of Last Order's head, she prescribed, "Not middle-aged, just *adults*, all right?"

"But how is getting angry at a little kid right away the adult thing to do, asks Mis— *Owww!!* Hey, you over there, I need help and also a towel! pleads Misaka pleads Misaka, trying to evoke a paternal response with her upturned eyes and stuff!!"

The stupid little brat was wailing about something, but Accelerator ignored her and closed the changing room door.

He sighed.

"I told them to be more freakin' cautious."

6

"And that's what happened, says Misaka says Misaka, delivering her report of the incident."

Last Order was in the passage right outside Yomikawa's apartment. She wore a men's button-down, the sleeves extending past her fingertips, over a sky-blue camisole.

The tiny girl was talking to someone who looked like a blown-up version of her: serial number 10032, Little Misaka.

Little Misaka was wearing the winter uniform of Tokiwadai, consisting of a beige blazer and a dark-blue checkered, pleated skirt. The Sisters wearing the same things as their original, Mikoto Misaka, was a convenience issue with the experiment, but even after the study ended, the mannerisms remained.

One difference between her and the original was the pair of large electronic goggles around Little Misaka's forehead. They were shaped like night vision goggles but were actually for visualizing information the naked eye couldn't see, like lines of magnetic force and electron rays.

Little Misaka watched Last Order closely, her eyes betraying no emotion. "Your report has already been sent through the network to all Misakas, so is there a need to repeat it verbally? asks Misaka, conducting a verification of her natural question."

"Sometimes we need to use our regular five senses to communicate so we can correct stuff like time miscalculations, says Misaka says Misaka, finding an excuse that seems reasonable!"

"If you say so, says Misaka, turning aside her superior's complaints with a tired look. It may also assist in Misaka's rehabilitation, says Misaka, forcing herself to search for elements to convince herself with."

She claimed her face looked tired, but her expression hadn't actually changed one millimeter. Last Order was flailing her hands and feet around, but Little Misaka wasn't overwhelmed by her excitement.

Instead, she looked up at the apartments in front of her, moving along at her own pace. "What a foolish situation, however, to have been standing aimlessly out here after being locked outside by an automated mechanism, says Misaka, offering an evaluation of the situation. I wonder how long you would have been alone had Misaka not coincidentally been taking a walk, says Misaka, smiling to herself as she doubts the host individual's specifications."

"It wasn't Misaka's fault, it was the auto-lock thing being very rude! says Misaka says Misaka in indignation! The electronic lock was being annoying and not letting Misaka's power work on it and making a really high-pitched beeping noise! says Misaka says Misaka, flailing her hands around to vent her stress and stuff!!"

"Is it not a praiseworthy state of affairs that it didn't budge even after using the power of an electromaster on it? says Misaka, offering an objective viewpoint."

Last Order groaned like a persistent dog. Unfortunately, the petite "network host individual" didn't know much about the wider world, and her interest at any given moment easily flitted from one thing to the other. "Also, I've been wondering, says Misaka says Misaka, pointing at your forehead."

"? Misaka's forehead is of average size, and Misaka is not a character known for her forehead, says Misaka, putting a hand to her forehead just to make sure."

"No, not that—those goggles, says Misaka says Misaka, pointing again." Last Order had her eyes on Little Misaka's electronic goggles. The small girl looked at her questioningly. "Um, how come all the other Misakas have a pair, but Misaka doesn't get any? says Misaka says Misaka, looking at you with envy."

Little Misaka seemed to just remember the goggles on her forehead and touched them with a fingertip. She looked at Last Order, who was staring up at her, saw she had no goggles on her forehead, and said, "Those Misakas are those Misakas, and this Misaka is this Misaka, says Misaka, tacitly suggesting that you give up."

"That's like when they say, 'Other families aren't like our family,' and that won't convince me! says Misaka says Misaka, immediately arguing! Besides, by that reasoning, Misaka is the only one who is part of a different family, says Misaka says Misaka, pointing out an even bigger problem and stuff!!"

She moaned and groaned between all her repetitions of the word *Misaka*. Then she grabbed Little Misaka's skirt and started angrily flapping it up and down.

"Misaka wants one, Misaka wants one! says Misaka says Misaka, employing a spoiled child's version of negotiation by using her tiny appearance to maximum effect!!"

"You may be attempting to act in a cute manner, but when used on a member of the same sex, it only makes them angry, having the opposite effect, explains Misaka concisely."

More importantly, with her skirt up like that, everyone could see the panties she was in the mood for today—ones tied on either side with a ribbon—but Little Misaka didn't seem to care about that part at all.

Last Order groaned in irritation at her stony expression. "Hey, number 10032, could you bow for a second? asks Misaka asks Misaka."

"?"

Though she was suspicious, Little Misaka decided to follow the host individual's instruction.

"Ha-ha-ha, you're wide open! says Misaka says Misaka, succeeding in her burglary!!"

She'd torn the goggles away from Little Misaka's bowed head.

Before her victim could say anything, Last Order turned around with a delighted grin and cried, "If you're falling for beginner's tricks like that, then maybe they need to check the routines used by all the network individuals, says Misaka says Misaka in parting! Come on, if you don't like it, try to get them back, says Misaka says Misaka, basking in her victory as she dashes away at breakneck speed!!"

Pat, pat, pat, pat, pat!! She scrambled away and disappeared more quickly than her appearance would suggest she could.

"..." Little Misaka stared after her in a daze for a few moments but soon snapped out of it. "Misaka cannot do anything about a direct order from the network host body, says Misaka with incredible reluctance while removing a submachine gun and rubber bullets, confirming the situation."

Ka-click!! rang the menacing metallic noise, echoing throughout the unmenacing city streets.

"*An exercise* though it may be, the opponent is the host individual, so it would not be childish for Misaka, a network node, to challenge her with everything Misaka has, says Misaka, offering a natural perspective. This is by no means Misaka getting mad, but merely exercising appropriate judgment based on logic, says Misaka, breaking into a sprint with her live firearm in one hand and praising herself for pretending that her own thought processes are level and calm."

With an expression that looked impassive, but upon closer inspection revealed her eyes twitching, Little Misaka began her pursuit.

Meanwhile, Last Order, who had caught on to Little Misaka's mentality, used the Misaka network—consisting of the Sisters' brain waves and weak electromagnetic waves—to provoke her pursuer as she ran through back roads.

"Ha-ha! No way a regular Misaka will beat this Misaka, says Misaka says Misaka, roaring with laughter at her victory over the lowly commoner!

"The time for revolution has come, declares Misaka number 10032, here and now."

INTERLUDE TWO

In London's Lambeth district was something like a girls' dormitory for Necessarius, the Church of Necessary Evils.

From the outside, it wasn't too different from the oft-seen stone-built apartments facing the roads. Unlike wooden structures, this one, made of stone, was hard to tell the age of at a glance; if someone told a person it had a centuries-long history, they probably couldn't imagine it from the exterior. It was just that well-kept and responsibly used.

It hadn't been turned into a fortress like Lambeth Palace, residence of the archbishop. Instead, it had been prepared as a building they could easily replace with a spare in case it was destroyed, though nobody could remember it ever being demolished before. It was not unlikely for enemy sorcerers' societies who discovered what the building really was to attempt mounting attacks on it…but any and all dangerous elements targeting the place had been sent to their graves before they could carry out their plans. The dorm was something that secretly displayed the military accomplishments of Necessarius. In other words, it was obvious bait.

Moving on.

It was early afternoon in Japan, but in London, night had fallen a while ago.

The districts away from the main streets, even in the capital city of

England, were once again veiled in the cradle of darkness, but there was a light on in one window, as if to symbolize someone having a late night.

It was the dressing room.

The space was quite large, given that it was adjacent to an expansive bathing area. In the corner sat a giant, empty cardboard box big enough to fit a school desk into. Product manuals and warranties were lined up on the floor.

As for what "product" the manuals were for—they were for washing machines.

And they had the words *Made in Academy City* printed on them.

Present were various electronic devices, very ill-matched with the ages-old dormitory.

"The archbishop...Why would she send us something so complex and troublesome?"

Hooking up the grounded wire with an agitated face was Kaori Kanzaki.

Her black hair was so long that even in a ponytail it reached down to her waist. Normally, she preferred an active outfit, like a short-sleeved T-shirt tied at the waist to bare her belly button or jeans with one leg cut off all the way up to the thigh. Right now, though, she wore a plain yukata. Her ridiculously long katana, however, was propped against a wall close at hand.

Until now, she'd been using a washing machine that rocked so hard when it turned on she always expected smoke to start coming out, but it had finally broken down earlier. Despite the archbishop's behavior, she seemed the type to listen to her subordinates' requests.

The new washing machine had arrived that evening. It was cutting-edge, fully automatic with an onboard AI, but neither Kanzaki nor any of the others ever handled machines much, so for them, it was almost an encounter with a mysterious supercivilization. She'd been tilting her head in confusion at the thing, scanning over the instruction manual again and again, and before she'd realized, it was quite late.

Incidentally, the reason she was so absorbed in her work was because they'd gotten a cardboard box Tsuchimikado sent from Japan that afternoon. After discovering a maid uniform plus a little extra (a fallen-angel costume set including a halo and wings), she would have done nearly anything to forget about it.

"Archbishop Laura said, 'With this *edge-cutting doohickey drum*, detestable cleaning work is as nothing at all!' but..."

Saying that with a smile was Orsola Aquinas. A sister who had been part of the Roman Orthodox Church until a few days ago, the woman was covered from hair to toenails in a black nun's habit. Her proportions were similar to Kanzaki's, but in contrast to the tight, lean impression Kanzaki gave off, Orsola seemed to have more of an emphasis on serenity.

Other former Roman Orthodox followers were present as well— the small and sassy Agnes Sanctis, the punctilious Lucia, and Angeline, who was weak against sweet foods and getting up in the morning.

They seemed to avoid simply converting to English Puritanism and had been throwing around the idea of making their own splinter of the Roman Orthodox Church since there were two hundred fifty of them anyway. If someone like Lidvia Lorenzetti, locked up in the Tower of London, were to hear that, bad things would follow. Given Laura Stuart's relatively laid-back approach to things, though, she seemed willing to accept them as a small religious order in their own right under her jurisdiction, like she had with the Amakusa Church.

Other than those five, Sherry Cromwell was also in the dressing room, a dyed-in-the-wool English Puritan. With damaged blond hair and light-brown skin, she was fond of regularly wearing gothic lolita fashion, but at the moment she wore a thin negligee. She had put on another set of pajamas over that, though, so while her curves could be *seen*, the details were rather unfairly hidden from view. It was on the same level as steam covering up all the sensitive bits at the bath.

Sherry, also a supervisor at the Royal Academy of the Arts, ignored their exchange, using an engraving knife to whittle down a small piece of marble and carving the contours of a chess piece out of it. The fine dust was assembling near her shoulder and forming a ball. Apparently, she was using her golem, Ellis, to do so.

With her eyes still down on her in-progress chess piece, she said, "Can't you just do your laundry in a river or something?"

"I would only need a washboard, but doing it in a river would cause environmental problems," replied Kanzaki, who had finished hooking up the grounding wires as she pushed the washing machine against the wall, the large device rattling as it went.

The scene didn't affect Sherry, who used Ellis for these things, and Kanzaki was incredibly strong, one of only twenty saints in the entire world. The others, though, winced a little.

"This thing…It was quite a pain to set up the earthquake-proof reinforcements and the anti–lightning strike equipment, but it seems just turning this one on shouldn't be an issue."

Blip. Kanzaki pressed a large button, but waiting for her were lines of countless numbers and symbols displayed on a small waterproof LCD screen.

She stared at it impassively for a moment. "…Can we not do this the honest way and wash things by hand?"

"N-no, no! Keep trying, just a little bit more!!"

Arguing in a half-crying state was Angeline, who was especially incompetent even among the rest of the group.

"Just a little more! A…a fully automatic washing machine is at our fingertips! My arms are going to fall off just from the temporary measure of carrying all our clothes to a washing machine in another building before this arrived!! I…I wouldn't even be able to wash them by hand now if I tried!!"

Judging by that arrangement and by the appearance of Angeline's small hands, she looked like she'd keel over the moment clothes-washing duty came back around to her.

Orsola looked down at the instruction manual. "Oh, Miss Kanzaki. From what I can see in the manual, you just press the button labeled Wash, and the machine will do everything else for you."

"?"

"If you put the detergent in this small box right here, the machine will analyze its composition, then automatically adjust the amount of water and detergent based on the weight of the clothing inside. It would seem it does everything, from pouring the water in, rinsing, draining, spinning, and drying."

"What an annoying contraption. We already measure the detergent, so it could have been even easier to operate."

But you just have to press one button, thought Agnes, Lucia, and Angeline at about the same time. Unfortunately, they were the newcomers here at the moment, so they stayed silent.

Orsola knocked on the new washing machine affectionately. "If it truly is as convenient as it says, I would very much like to see it in action."

"…Orsola, it's already the middle of the night," said Kanzaki, exasperated. "Should we be using a washing machine at this hour?"

Once again, the sister pointed to the manual. "It says here that it's designed to be soundproof and that it's okay to run at night."

"There's stuff here about phones and decibels. Do you actually understand this? In any case, today's laundry is already stored away, isn't it?"

This dorm was for the female members of Necessarius. Their clothing, even down to its patterns and individual stitches, was all magically enhanced. Their clothing could be considered both weapons and armor for them, and if they just dropped them all in a laundry basket, all the defensive mechanisms could have unintended, violent interactions. There were certain affinities in terms of the spell's religion or school, too, but it was now a fundamental rule to take that into consideration during washing, too.

Sherry, still whittling away at her chess piece, said in vague annoyance, "The vault is protected by a triple-layered magical lock, isn't it? It'd take forever to get through 'em all, and it'd be even *worse* to set it all back up again."

Kanzaki's face lit up as though she'd gotten her way. She stood up straight. "See? We don't have anything to wash, so we can't use the washing machine. We're getting up early again tomorrow, so let's just turn out the lights and get to sleep now."

"Oh, but we have laundry to be done right here."

No sooner had Orsola made her declaration than she began to unreservedly strip off the habit she was wearing.

Kanzaki looked at her, aghast. "Y-you don't need to make more laundry on purpose! Such acts will have a negative influence on the newcomers as well. Agnes, and the rest of you, your faces look like you're wondering if this is a custom, but it's not, so please don't go along with Orsola's actions!!"

"Now, now. Japan's yukatas are made to be very easy to take off. The obis are dyed in a very pretty way, too."

"I'd prefer it if you listened to me and didn't suddenly grab my belt like that!!"

By the time Kanzaki tried to stop her, the indigo-dyed belt around her waist had already come undone and fallen to the floor. The front of her yukata opened up like all the buttons on a coat popping off.

Orsola's eyes widened. "Kanzaki, are you the sort who doesn't wear any underwear?"

"You're not supposed to with yukatas!!"

She hid her body with both hands imbued with the explosive physical strength of a saint, so even Orsola couldn't steal the actual yukata away from her.

With nothing more to do, Orsola threw her own habit and that of the other sisters—who were saying things like "Wait, what're we supposed to wear to bed?" and "Sister Agnes, you will inevitably end up in your underwear as soon as you grow tired anyway"—along with Kanzaki's yukata obi, into the washing machine. She closed the see-through lid and pressed the big button labeled Wash.

It was silent as promised. As the water poured into the tub inside, the contents began to spin around, without so much as shaking the machine. The tub seemed to be spherical, rather than the oil-drum-shaped sort of yesteryear; it rotated in 360-degree space. Just watching it made the machine seem amazing.

"Oh my, it really is quiet!" said Orsola like a kid intently watching a roller coaster. The others, like Agnes and Angeline, were also examining the washing machine's operation from over her shoulders. They were treating it like people used to treat color televisions in the old days. It was extremely weird how they were all in their underwear, though.

"...You stole my belt just so you could see this?" Only Kanzaki was disheartened as she hung her head.

But suddenly, Sherry said to her, "Hey, Far Eastern religious sect person."

"I'm currently nothing but a retired ninja, but what is it?"

"The manual. Did you read it?"

Kanzaki looked at her again in confusion. The brown-skinned, two-layer-negligee-wearing woman sighed as she moved her engraving knife, using it to point to the instruction manual on the floor.

"Well, it says here there's a different setting for clothes that can bleed color and to separate them from regular laundry. Is your dyed obi going to be all right?"

"Gyaaahhh!!" screamed Kanzaki as she attacked the washing machine.

The saint gave it a fierce look, like she was going to punch it. All four of the former Roman Orthodox sisters used their complete strength to hold her back, but Kaori Kanzaki, using her incredible physical abilities, slipped through them all and grabbed the machine near the control panel.

"S-stop it! Where's the button to stop the washing?!"

She glanced around the panel in a frenzy, searching. But she was never very good with machines, and the chaos didn't help, either. The button should have been right there, but she didn't even know where to begin.

Meanwhile, the washing machine kept on spinning.

Orsola, watching the tub through the clear lid, cried out in delight. "Miss Kanzaki, it is clearly washing all the stains from your obi!!"

"No, it's just making it fade! You stupid vanguard of scientific civilization!!"

Kanzaki finally couldn't stand it any longer. Even though the machine was still going, she ripped the clear lid off, mostly by force.

But inside was a cutting-edge spherical 360-degree rotating washing machine tub.

Before she had time to blink, water suddenly able to escape the centrifugal force splashed Kaori Kanzaki, causing her clothes to become see-through.

"W-wow. You really aren't wearing any..."

A moment after Angeline's careless remark, the former priestess actually yelled at her, then broke down crying.

CHAPTER 3

Misaka and Misaka's Little Sisters
Sister_and_Sisters.

1

Touma Kamijou sat down on a bench in a small plaza (nonsmoking) in the underground mall meant for meeting up with people, drinking his small two hundred–milliliter bottle of oolong tea.

He was all alone for the moment.

Kuroko Shirai, who had been around here until a short time ago after Mikoto Misaka shoved her away, had disappeared somewhere with her teleport ability, shouting, "I only did what I did out of consideration for you, Big Sister! To think my kindness would turn into a double-edged sword…!!" Despite the interruption, Mikoto had returned to the service store to finish her cell phone sign-up paperwork or something. Kamijou had actually been with her the first time, but they'd left in the middle. Incidentally, the peculiar ace of Tokiwadai Middle School was inside the shop right now, eyes glittering after she learned she could get a Croaker *and* a Hoppit at the same time. It was a pain to talk to people in that state, though, so being away from her was the better option.

"…I hope she calms down soon." Kamijou sighed, glancing at his cell phone screen. It was hard to tell since they were underground, but it was already past four in the afternoon. There was a lot of paperwork and forms to fill out, after all, but he still couldn't help thinking about how much time this errand had taken.

Then, as he relaxed on the bench, Mikoto Misaka returned.

"Hey, you're done already?" asked Kamijou.

In response, Mikoto stayed silent for some reason and turned her face slightly aside. She looked like she could have been hesitating, but he didn't remember doing anything to make her worry over a simple answer. He crooked his head. "What? What happened? Oh, you're not carrying a bag with your new cell phone in it or anything. Did something come up?"

"N-no, Misaka is…" Mikoto waved her hands around in a smooth motion that produced no noise, then eventually put a hand to her forehead. "…This Misaka is the Misaka who is usually wearing goggles, says Misaka, informing you of her serial code of number 10032 so you can reassess the situation."

"Wait, are you Little Misaka?"

Little Misaka nodded briskly.

She had the same body as Mikoto Misaka down to her hair follicles, so maybe nobody could blame him for getting them confused. Rugged-looking night vision goggles always sat on her forehead, but for some reason she didn't have them today.

Something unique seemed to be going on with her today as well. "…Have you seen a Misaka who is about this size? asks Misaka, placing her palm horizontally a little below her chest."

She was describing a height about the same as Komoe or a little shorter. As Kamijou watched her gestures, his expression became dubious. "You guys can change your sizes and stuff?"

"Based on your reaction, you don't seem to know, says Misaka, disillusioned with your uselessness while continuing to calculate that asshole's escape route."

Little Misaka sighed slightly. As she readjusted her schoolbag, Kamijou heard a dull, metallic *click* from inside.

She's not too happy again, thought Kamijou.

She continued, "To put it plainly, Misaka's goggles have been stolen, reports Misaka with a grim face. Without those goggles, it is difficult to distinguish between Misaka and the original, so I must recover them as soon as possible—but my current situation could be called very disadvantageous, says Misaka, secretly asking for help with upturned eyes."

"..."

That high-handedness seemed to be shared between the older and younger Sisters. He made a face. "Yeah, you could be mistaken for Mikoto like that, huh?"

"Yes, affirms Misaka in response. Earlier, while running down a street with a submachine gun in one hand, I was suddenly shouted at by a female student in twin tails and had a rough time, says Misaka, seriously describing a tale of hardship."

"Err…Twin tails…"

Kamijou had an inkling who that person might have been, but he could only pray she didn't harm Mikoto's daily life in any way. And he thought he heard a dangerous term mixed in there—*submachine gun?*—but hoping it was only something he misheard was all he could manage.

"Anyway, you probably want something to tell you apart from Mikoto, at least until you get your goggles back."

"Are you telling Misaka to become a forehead character? wonders Misaka."

"Wipe that term from your memory right now." *Who taught her that?* thought Kamijou in all seriousness. "It doesn't have to be your forehead. Hmm. You're wearing the exact same uniform, too… What if you just took off your blazer?"

"I was not aware you had the hobby of demanding people remove their clothing in public, says Misaka, not quite understanding the benefit but following your instruction for now."

"Pfft?! Why did you suddenly put your hands on your skirt?! I get it, I get it! Don't take anything off— Hey, how about you put on an accessory instead that should make you stand out?!!"

"I have no decorations of the sort on hand, and purchasing one seems costly, says Misaka, making an appeal to her domestic nature with a practical response."

I'm gonna have to ask that frog-faced doctor about their living environment at some point, Kamijou promised to himself. "Well, there's a whole world of different accessories out there. It's fine as long as people can tell you apart. I'm sure you could buy *something* with one thousand yen at a place around here. I mean, if it was that cheap, I'd buy it for you."

"You'd buy…?"

"But what? A girl talking about accessories…Maybe a ring would work."

"…A ring."

For some reason, Little Misaka fell silent.

Kamijou didn't notice at all. "Actually, a ring probably wouldn't stand out enough. Gotta be something that really tells the world, you know? Maybe a skull mask would— *Oww?!*"

As soon as he reconsidered, he received a punch from the expressionless Little Misaka.

2

"The stupid brat disappeared?"

Accelerator's voice echoed in the big living room.

He was pretty sure Last Order was in her specifically assigned room taking a nap or something, but according to Yomikawa, she wasn't in the apartment.

The tracksuit-wearing woman shook her head a little. "This place has auto-locks like in hotels, so if you just want to go outside, you don't need a key. So I'm thinking she might have gone out to play on her own."

"This is a big complex, so she could also be playing in an elevator or stairs or a hallway," Yoshikawa supposed.

Accelerator had a bad feeling about this.

He didn't believe the optimistic idea that human nature was fundamentally good. He'd come across far too much evil in his life for that.

…When did I last see the squirt?

He looked at the clock hanging on the wall.

The current time was four thirty PM. It could have been one or two in the afternoon when he woke up from his post-lunch nap and tried to shower.

Two hours at the most, I guess. With that much time, a pro could've killed her, buried the body, and gotten away.

Accelerator and Last Order were alike in that they were both incredibly valuable research specimens. The "experiment" they'd been entangled in was suspended at the moment, but it wouldn't be strange at all for someone else to come up and try to use the research for their own gain.

Actually, he didn't need to put it in terms of net gain or calculations. Someone could have just said, "I'm an acquaintance of the Accelerator" and marked him for some kind of attack. Now that he'd lost the title of Academy City's strongest, he was nothing more than a target.

Accelerator sucked his teeth loudly in frustration, then adjusted the modern crutch holding him up. "I'm going out."

"Well, I think she's just playing around nearby, yeah?" Yomikawa remarked in an awfully relaxed tone, causing him to shoot her an angry glare. "I mean, she left a message on the answering machine."

"..." Accelerator quieted, then pressed the message playback button on the rather large home answering machine sitting next to the phone, fax machine, and copier.

After a shrill, electronic *beep*, "Um, Misaka is playing tag with one of the Misaka network nodes right now, reports Misaka reports Misaka. I can't come back right away, but I hope you make some dinner for me, requests Misaka requests Misaka and stuff."

He attempted to slam on the phone with his crutch before Yomikawa and Yoshikawa held him back. Without his ability, all he could do was flail around helplessly.

Now that his hair and clothes were messed up, Accelerator, gasping for breath, muttered, "...Most annoying brat on the face of the planet."

"Ah-ha-ha," laughed Yomikawa. "That's how relationships work."

She left her arms tightly around his torso, afraid he might still try to break the phone. In that position, her big chest pressed against him, but he didn't seem to care at all.

"You won't find any relationships that are always convenient for you, 'kay? Being free and nobody getting in your way—all that really means is that nobody will notice you no matter what you do." She let her arms down. "That's what it means to take root somewhere. The more you interact, the harder it is to do things. But you'll be just that much stronger against the winds and rain."

"..."

Listening to adults' opinions was such a pain.

He wished she'd do something about these lectures—they could be completely on point or absolute misses.

In any event, Accelerator decided it would be a better idea to find Last Order and keep her where he could see her. He was free to act thanks to the weak electromagnetic waves sent and received by the electrodes on his neck, but Last Order was the one at the heart of the Sisters' activity. He still didn't understand what the Misaka network was like—not logically, yet he got the gist of it in a sensory way—but if something hampered the network node individuals' activity, it could affect him as well. Yes, this was all completely for his own sake.

Meanwhile, Yomikawa wore a slightly triumphant look, as though she thought she'd said something good. "Anyway, Kikyou and I will help."

"Me too?"

"If you don't want to, then you've gotta give up the name Kikyou."

Yoshikawa looked out the window, not appearing to be ready for much physical activity. "I'll collapse if I walk for more than an hour outside in one day...," she muttered.

Accelerator frowned. "The hell are you talking about?"

"We're gonna go look for her, right?" said Yomikawa like it was obvious, causing Accelerator to fall silent for a moment.

Meanwhile, the tracksuit-wearing woman took the USB memory stick out of the answering machine. "Looks like she's not in the building, but if we analyze the background noise in the message, we can figure out where to look, yeah? You can just leave everything to the nice Anti-Skill lady!"

"Aiho, don't abuse your position."

"Searching for and locating lost children is one of our jobs as keepers of the peace. No problem, right?"

Why the hell does she look like she's having fun? Accelerator thought.

Yomikawa grinned at him, the memory stick in her hand. "This is called a mutually beneficial relationship, 'kay?"

"You mean tripping over each other's feet?"

"It's scratching each other's backs," Yoshikawa said with a sigh as they set up their Last Order search net.

3

Little Misaka was in a very irritable mood.

In a corner of the underground mall, Touma Kamijou was trembling in constant fear.

In the end, he'd bought her a cheap necklace that came to exactly one thousand yen after consumption tax, but he was beginning to think there was another source causing this state of anger. Sometimes she would fidget and mumble things like "a ring..." and "Misaka's ring finger on her left hand..." What could she possibly have been worrying about?

"Um, Little Misaka?"

"..."

"If you don't like the necklace that much, then we can return it..."

"...Please do not steal anything more from Misaka, says Misaka in a soft but serious voice."

...So she likes the actual necklace, right? wondered Kamijou. He couldn't even guess what she was agonizing over. Plus, he was starting to think about Mikoto, since she hadn't come back out of the store yet. And now Little Misaka was like this. When it rains, it pours.

Anyway, I should try to cheer her up, Kamijou considered, flustered, looking around. "Hmm? They're selling sweets. Let's eat some, Little Misaka."

The reason he immediately diverted the conversation to the topic of food was probably because of the pure-white sister Index's influence. *That's not a reflex I'm proud of,* he thought with self-disgust.

Meanwhile, Misaka looked at him, face blank. "Trying to buy me with gifts, are you? says Misaka, attempting a frank assertion."

"Ahh?!"

"However, you took such action in consideration for Misaka, so Misaka will respect your intent, says Misaka, deciding to take you up on your kindness."

Well, Kamijou had her stamp of approval, so he headed for the store.

It was a small store the size of an ice cream shop, its counter right up to the mall path. They sold small pastries shaped like animals such as baby birds and puppies. They looked somewhat like octopus balls, *takoyaki*, but they were probably made of hotcake dough and filled with custard cream. They were like the fish-shaped sweets, *tai-yaki*, but using western fillings like cheese and custard.

The animal patterns were created directly from molds on a black metal pan.

Behind the counter stood a smiling older girl who looked like she was in college. "Do you know what you'd like?"

"Do different animals have different flavors? Like different fillings?"

"No, not at all. If we don't make them all the same, we can't collect data."

"...?"

"Well, you know how people will unconditionally like certain designs just for how they look or feel for no logical reason? If you figure that out, you can apply it to fields like clothing and makeup. This is like a survey where we tally up how many of each animal gets chosen."

Kamijou took a step back and looked at the store's signboard again.

The signboard made the store obviously look like a rental, and it had a university's name clearly written on it.

"Well, I guess there's no harm in it…Which should I choose? I think the baby bird will be good."

"Coming right up. You're the fifty-fourth one to choose it. Come again!"

Kamijou took it, but never stopped wondering about whether fifty-four sales of one product meant it was selling well or not.

In the transparent packaging, there were two rows of chicks, with five per row for a total of ten. Melted caramel topped the hotcake-like, yellow dough. Instead of toothpicks, the snack came with two small plastic forks.

"Here, Little Misaka. Eat up."

"…"

Kamijou put the package in front of her, offering it, but Little Misaka had stopped dead in her tracks, staring at the baby birds.

Actually, it looked more like she was meeting their eyes.

"Um, Little Misaka…?"

"…" She didn't respond.

Without changing her expression, she began sucking her teeth in a soft *chee, chee, chee* sound.

Come to think of it, Little Misaka has less experience with the world than me, and I'm an amnesiac. Maybe she doesn't know how to eat them.

For some reason, she was poking at the baby birds' beaks with a slender finger, saying something along the lines of "Hmm, what clever birds not to bite me, sighs Misaka in admiration."

Eventually, Kamijou picked up one of the plastic forks. Then, to lecture Little Misaka, he poked the fork's prongs into the back of one of the birds as a test.

Little Misaka gave a huge jolt. "Th-the birdy's little round body is…?! says Misaka in trepidation…Why is that one so obedient? wonders Misaka, since the bird isn't even chirping."

"Huh? What's been going on with you, Little Misaka? If you don't want them, I'll eat them all."

"E-eat them…?!"

As she continued being all fluttery for some reason, Kamijou dubiously put one of the birds in his mouth. When he munched on the soft dough, the expected western pastry–style sweetness spread through his mouth.

"Hey, this thing is pretty good for a trial product."

Meanwhile, Little Misaka had her eyes glued to the bird's dotted eyes (made of chocolate) inside the boy's mouth, and she received quite a shock.

"………………………………………………………………………Ev…"

While listening to the sounds of munching, she still watched the bird's cute face, which looked like it wanted to say something, as it continued to be chewed to bits.

Little Misaka's whole body was trembling. "Even if it is a trial product! says Misaka, saving the bird's liiiiiiiiiiiiiiiiiiiiiiiiiiiiife!!"

"*Mghfhr?!* Wh-what are you going crazy and sparking around for all of a—?"

Before Kamijou could finish shouting, pale blue sparks sprayed from Little Misaka's body.

She was Radio Noise—an electrical fault.

Even twenty thousand of them together wouldn't have strength enough to rival the Railgun.

But he still couldn't underestimate her.

One twenty-thousandth of a billion volts was still fifty thousand volts.

"Bwah?!"

Unluckily for him, Kamijou had a fork in his left hand and the package of baby birds in his right. In other words, his hands were completely tied—and that's when the fifty-thousand-volt attack hit him.

Even Imagine Breaker couldn't deal with that.

The surprise attack sent Kamijou tumbling down to the underground mall floor.

Students moving through the passage whispered among themselves, saying, "Whoa!" and "Did you see that spark just now?!"

"Hah?! cries Misaka, seeing the birds scattered about and coming to her senses!!"

Brought back to normal not by Kamijou, but by the birds—she must have really been obsessed with the things.

She picked up the clear, upside-down package and immediately began returning the baby birds to it.

Her face was the definition of seriousness.

Meanwhile, Kamijou stumbled off the floor a few steps away and up to his feet. "Urgh…Sorry, Little Misaka…"

He apologized, so Little Misaka listened to him as she cradled the package of birds in both hands.

Touma Kamijou spoke. "…Sorry for wasting food like that. But I'll still eat them even if they fell on the floor because of the three-second rule."

As he finished talking, Little Misaka kicked him across the floor.

She was breathing heavily and was quite angry now. He couldn't quite figure out what she was thinking. He guessed she must have really been hungry.

Then…

As he stood there full of question marks, another familiar face approached.

"Uh…What the heck are you two doing?!"

It was Mikoto Misaka, who was looking more at Little Misaka and trotting up to her than Kamijou. In addition to her school-bag, she was carrying a small paper packet with the phone company logo on it. She shouldn't have swapped her phone itself, but the paperwork, expansion chip, and mascot straps and stuff were probably in there. Convenience stores and supermarkets had been refraining voluntarily from wasting bags on every little purchase, but it didn't look like the service store had started any such activities.

"Still, though…," Kamijou mused aloud.

Mikoto Misaka and Little Misaka.

He really couldn't tell the difference when they stood next to each other. Nevertheless, twins were nothing unusual, so maybe the people going by in the mall were paying more attention to the Tokiwadai brand. They looked exactly alike, but Little Misaka had a necklace so he wouldn't mix them up. Thank goodness for that.

Little Misaka answered Mikoto's question. "Misaka has traveled far to come to this underground mall to recover the goggles stolen from her, replies Misaka, her eyes drawn to the original's frog mascot. Processing Misaka serial number 20001's predicted escape route as well as a list of firearms for intercepting her, but Misaka is so engrossed in the frog now that she doesn't care anymore, says Misaka, giving up."

"Could you please actually explain?!"

Angry, Mikoto put her Croaker and Hoppit into her schoolbag. Little Misaka's face didn't change much, but a tinge of sadness crept into her eyes. She looked down at the bag of baby birds in her hands and thought for a moment. "Misaka will not cheat on you, says Misaka, reaffirming the birds in her hands."

"Cheat on...What are you talking about?" said Mikoto, giving up. Still, she seemed to have her own interest in the birds' design.

But Little Misaka gripped them tighter to her chest with both hands. "The original should just stay addicted to her frogs, says Misaka, creating an ironclad defense as though she would take the birds with her to the grave."

"Mgh. Come on, you could at least just let me look at them."

"Misaka cannot, and that is final, says Misaka, carrying through with her intent. If you want them so much, then just have him there buy them for you like Misaka did, says Misaka, gesturing with her chin."

Mikoto spun around to look at Kamijou.

"..." She stayed silent for a few moments, then finally took a deep breath and said, "We were talking about how you lost our bet and had to do anything I said for the punishment game, weren't we?"

"Huh? What?"

"...You're specifically assigned to Miss Mikoto and have to stay with her the entire day because of that, right? You're going to do everything you can, with all your energy, like your life depends on it, right?"

"Why?! Why does the air around you seem like it's charged right now?!"

"Because even at times like this, you never, ever change!! You go up and talk to all these random people during *my* punishment game. I didn't know you liked the sound of a *little sister* so much, you boneheaaaaaaaaaaaaaaad!!"

A billion volts of electricity flew from her bangs, but Kamijou swung his right fist up to repel them. After repeating the process two or three times, she yelled, "Argh, this is ticking me off!! How can you endure all that?! I wish you'd just let it blast you away once in a while!!"

"What the hell are you angry about?! Besides, if I accepted your request, it'd kill me!!"

She eventually realized how unproductive this was after another ten or twenty tries. Mikoto was fatigued and stopped attacking him with lightning. Kamijou was, for his part, on the verge of collapse; the mall was filled with voices saying, "Hey, should we call Anti-Skills?" and "No, I don't want to get involved"; and Little Misaka was poking at the pastry birds' beaks with her index finger.

Suddenly she looked up from the chicks. "By the way, what is the original doing here? asks Misaka, beginning information collection."

"Huh?!" Mikoto's shoulders gave a violent jolt. It wasn't like she and Kamijou were doing anything special, but Mikoto looked away from Little Misaka for some reason. "W-well, we had a little bet for a punishment game during the Daihasei Festival and I won, and as the winner, I'm just dragging this idiot around, that's all. Er, um, maybe I should have explained the festival first. Basically, it's like—"

"In other words, the original isn't able to be honest with herself, says Misaka, beginning information analysis."

"Pfft?! What information did you get, and how did you analyze it to come to that conclusion?! I—I don't have any ulterior motives.

Be honest with myself? I'm not even sure what you're talking about! Besides, what would you want me to do if I was honest with myself? To this bonehead?!"

As Mikoto shoved her finger toward Kamijou's face, Little Misaka didn't bat an eyelash. "Hmm, Misaka doesn't understand why you are treating him so brusquely, argues Misaka. Misaka owes her life to this person, so he doesn't deserve such treatment, says Misaka, unflinchingly seeking correction."

"Urk...B-but that doesn't have anything to do with the current situation, does it? What's wrong with calling this bonehead a bonehead?"

"I see—you continue to be dishonest, says Misaka, reaching a final confirmation."

Little Misaka gave one close look into Mikoto's eyes.

"Then Misaka will be honest, says Misaka, choosing to walk a different path from the original."

As soon as she said that...

...she walked next to Kamijou and promptly hugged his right arm. Her meager chest pushed against his elbow.

"Dwahhh?!"

Kamijou felt his heart almost explode.

The purehearted boy nearly suffered respiratory distress from the immediate shock, but because of his panic, he couldn't see Mikoto's jaw silently moving up and down. Nearby male students spared occasional glances at them, but he was utterly unaware of them, too.

"Wha...wha...whaa...?"

As Mikoto watched in astonishment, Little Misaka, still clinging to Kamijou's right arm, nestled herself in closer. "Oops, says Misaka, casually moving the accessory he bought for her into the original's sight."

"?!"

Criiick came a strange sound from Mikoto's head.

Little Misaka was about to press her attack...

...when *tap, tap, grab!!*

"Misaka wants to hug him from the other side, says Misaka says Misaka, joining in because it seems fun!! Yaaay!!"

This time, a girl who looked about ten was hanging off his left arm.

Shocked, Kamijou looked over to find that though her body was young, her face looked exactly like Mikoto's. She had the same goggles on as the ones Little Misaka owned, but the rubber band was so loose, they ended up hanging from around her neck instead of on her forehead.

"Who is this?! Little sister of a little sister?!" asked Kamijou, bothered by the feeling of hardness that went beyond just being "meager."

But before he could get a response...

"Serial number 20001, you have guts to show your face so casually in front of Misaka, says Misaka, shifting into serious mode."

"Heh-heh-heh, Misaka is already tired of that game, says Misaka says Misaka, going off to dig up her next form of entertainment."

"You think you can escape?! shouts Misaka, taking her submachine gun out of her bag!"

Jagkk!! came the metallic noise, causing Mikoto to sputter. The overly small girl, in the meantime, disappeared into the crowd of people.

After pushing the baby birds softly to Kamijou and whispering to him, "If you treat them poorly, I will beat you to death, warns Misaka," she charged into the crowds with her submachine gun, which *really* didn't look like a toy.

He could hear their voices from the other side of the wall.

"That's you getting serious—how laughable! says Misaka says Misaka, making fun of you and stuff."

"This is where the real fun begins, says Misaka, deploying into her final full boost form!!"

Clack crack clackack-crack!! came successive strange metallic sounds from past the crowds like someone was building something. Kamijou sort of wanted to take a look, but he was also scared, so he vowed not to get near them.

4

Five PM.

After leaving the air-conditioned apartment, Accelerator set his crutch on the asphalt. His other hand was already holding a cell phone.

In the end, they'd decided to look for Last Order, since she still hadn't returned yet.

Today was apparently a half day for classes all around Academy City, but at this hour, things were no different than a normal weekday. To break in their newly made winter uniforms, the people walking around nearby were mostly wearing sailor uniforms and button-downs with stand-up collars and the like. If Accelerator had to pick out one difference, it would be the faint smell peculiar to new clothing wafting around.

"This goddamn weather...," muttered Accelerator at random, looking at the sky. He hadn't noticed since he'd been inside, but the blue sky was now gray—actually, it was almost black it was so cloudy. It might start raining any second. Because the Tree Diagram, Academy City's supercomputer used for organizing atmospheric data, had been destroyed, meteorologists hadn't been able to predict afternoon showers and other sudden weather changes lately.

"Ack. Let's find her and get home before it rains, yeah?"

He heard Yomikawa's voice through the phone; she must have been looking at the sky, too. Yoshikawa was minding the house. Last Order could always go back to the apartment during the search, so if they were all out, she'd be stuck standing at the front door since she didn't have a key or pass code.

He sucked his teeth. It would be great if standing there stuck was all that happened, but the probability of her waiting in front of the apartment was low, given how she would run across the city if she had the time. If she got bored, she'd leave, and that could make the search more difficult than it needed to be.

Accelerator adjusted the cell phone in his hand. "But you're in a freakin' car."

"I don't want to get wet while I open the door and put my umbrella up, 'kay?"

How feeble, he thought, but he refrained from insulting her out loud. After all, he was the one whose skin color was white because the sun's ultraviolet rays had never touched him. "Anyway, you get an idea of where that brat is?"

"The noise in the background sounded like the indoor music in the underground mall nearby."

"Eh? You used that analysis gear just to look for a lost kid? Don't you use that for crimes?"

"I told you. Looking for lost children is part of our job, 'kay? Uh, anyway. I've got a read on her location from analyzing the music in the background of her phone call."

"Hah. You talkin' about those *sounds people can't hear* going through the city?"

"Wow, didn't think anyone would catch on. More precisely, they're low-frequency waves, below human hearing range."

Idiot, Accelerator thought. He was an esper who could observe, calculate, and manipulate any vector one threw at him. If he let things he couldn't see or hear through, he wouldn't be able to block radiation.

"They're secretly mixed in with the background music in stores and stuff, right?"

"Yeah. Just those waves don't mean anything, but if you combine them with special frequency waves we Anti-Skill officers have, they turn into an actual sound. It's set up so every speaker emits a different noise, and if you look it up, you can basically find out where the person called from. After all, you can easily buy a device to mess with reverse searches these days, so the process requires effort."

Yomikawa then added stuff about this being only one search method and usually having to get more than one angle on the data by using a bunch at once.

What an annoying system. Accelerator sighed.

Being able to set up such rude systems without difficulty was one characteristic of Academy City. There were probably still many problems with it, like needing to revise the system and changing how to distribute equipment, but all those could be summed up with *Well, it's an experiment* and pushed through anyway.

"Anyway, I'm going to the underground mall now, right?"

"For now, yes. The rascal probably won't stay in one place very long, so you'll need to start asking around once you arrive."

"...Me? Accelerator? Like *this*?"

"Yes, now smile, practice your smile."

Are you stupid? Accelerator sucked his teeth. He was just too famous—in a bad way. If he, a Level Five esper, tried to *smile* and talk to someone, it could put the person into a state of shock. He wouldn't blame them for thinking they were about to be murdered and then shooting him on the spot. And honestly, he couldn't do anything about that. So he'd just have to kill them first.

Even so, he needed information to search for Last Order.

"This is gonna be a fucking pain," he muttered under his breath.

Then Yomikawa suddenly spoke. "Hey, Accelerator?"

"What?"

"Are you really that scared of being nice to people?"

"...Great, another delightful conversation. Perfect for an after-school walk, I'll tell ya."

"Must be nice being a tyrant."

Yomikawa wasn't listening.

Actually, she heard him, and now she was ignoring him.

"Well, everyone's got their own troubles, but there's gotta be something brighter in there. Tyrants never get betrayed, yeah? Don't have to worry about friendships ending. Don't have to fear others pushing your goodwill away. You're just a target of fear and hatred, after all."

The words came smoothly. Accelerator listened to them.

"I'm not gonna say you can only make relationships by being nice or being mean. That'd be too simple. But until now, all you had to do was push aside that rejection and ill will. And that's a fact. That was easy. Now things are different, though. That's why I'm asking, 'kay? Are you that afraid of choosing whether to be nice or mean to someone?"

"This is bullshit. I—"

"It's a fact," interrupted Yomikawa. "You accept all of Last Order's friendliness, but you're afraid of showing her your own. Your relationship might look positive, but it's actually a precarious one—because if that supply of friendliness from Last Order goes away, you can't bond with her."

Her voice was flat. Because she didn't place emphasis anywhere, she sounded relaxed, and that lent credence to her words.

"Accelerator, are you afraid to act because you don't know how to close the distance and because she might go farther away? Are you afraid that if your actions go wrong and that distance increases, that you'll never be able to put it back to normal? But if you don't act, you can't try."

"Lecturing me?"

"I know it's not my style, but I *am* still a teacher, 'kay? Anyway, I'm a low-level Anti-Skill officer, so *I probably won't have the chance to learn about your darkness.*"

Oh. Accelerator understood.

She already knew who he was—she'd probably looked into the city's data banks.

And she'd hit a wall, which was why she asked him directly now.

"That was a roundabout way of doing things."

"The place you were before…Well, the names being what they were…"

"The EEMA, yeah?"

Accelerator flatly spoke the name Yomikawa hesitated to say aloud.

It was the name of a facility, one recorded in an especially tight part of the data banks, sealed away from everyone.

"Its full name is the Exceptional Esper Multi-Adjustment Tech Lab. The 'school' they threw me into until I was nine and a hell where they disposed of dead bodies, people would say."

School and *dead bodies* were words that shouldn't have gone together at all; it was unique to Academy City. A lot of schools here also served as Ability Development institutions and testing labs. When rumors like that branched off, one got stories about "murderous" facilities that "conducted inhumane research."

"That place was actually worse than the rumors. It was no body-disposing site. It was the opposite—a rubbish heap for disposing of living people. I'm sure you've at least heard the rumors?"

"...Yes, I suppose."

The EEMA mainly did research and experimentation regarding double espers, or espers with more than one ability. Right now, students could only use a single ability, and the general consensus stated that using two or more at once was impossible. The data used for that conclusion, though, had mainly been collected at this lab.

In other words, it was a series of "failures" that went on forever until they discovered the rule.

Ability Development even used suggestive techniques and drugs, and its process directly affected brain structure—it was better not to imagine the tragedies the word *failure* implied. One would discover the true meaning behind the silly phrase *better off dead*.

Yomikawa spoke. "My unit was the one that pacified it and took it apart."

"Gee, thanks."

"They'd probably discovered the rule near the end—that espers can only have one ability. But they were after honor. They *wanted* a completed double esper, and they sacrificed a lot of children to do it. Especially using the Child Error."

Child Error was a societal phenomenon in Academy City.

The city was mostly made up of dormitories, and it was a general rule that one lived inside the city, even if they did so outside the dorms, such as freeloading in a bread shop in the city or something. But in rare cases, people would pay the Academy City matriculation fees just to abandon the child, make sure they got into a dormitory, and disappear completely. It was better than stuffing a little kid into a coin-operated locker, but it was essentially the same thing.

Academy City had a system in place to secure children like that.

Unfortunately, it *also* had parasitic research teams that took advantage of them. PRODUCE, Project Dark May, the Explosion Experiment for Analyzing Runaway Ability Laws…That was how research that even the progressive city wouldn't allow still happened anyway.

"…I saw it, too—what was lying behind those heavy doors." Yomikawa's voice was grave.

Accelerator smiled. It was normal to think *that was where the bottom of hell was.*

Her poor powers of imagination were proof that Aiho Yomikawa lived in a healthy world.

Unlike Accelerator, who smiled, knowing everything.

"Unfortunately, I didn't get to see your grand actions. Like I said, I was only there until I was nine. Then they moved me. You wanna know why?"

Accelerator's lips curled down.

"Because they couldn't handle me. Even that nightmarish place, the EEMA, couldn't handle my power. Even those devils in white lab coats feared me. That's the kind of monster I am," the white student said into the cell phone. "It was the same afterward, too. Bullshit. The Imaginary Number Facility, the Wisdom Labs, the Kirigaoka Attachment…It goes so deep, you've only seen the tip of the iceberg. But the response was the same wherever I went. The tragedies there were actually pretty *lame.* That's why I went through 'em so fast. Nobody could keep me there, so I just sank deeper and deeper."

Accelerator stomped his crutch. Its tip hit the asphalt as though he'd spat on the ground.

"I was never in the same place for more than two months. Every time, I was reminded of how much of a monster I am. They were all devils in the flesh, sure, but even *they* were scared of me. So what does that make me, eh?"

That was how the monster, whom nobody could deal with, ran out of places to go and ended up with the Level Six labs where Yoshikawa worked. He was treated totally different there, and that, among other things, kept him nearby for more than two months. But it was all just an inverted version of their fear toward Accelerator. It was written all over their faces—they didn't want to get him angry. About the only one who wasn't like that was the "soft" Yoshikawa.

Even the researchers who ended up massacring over ten thousand people in the end, their reaction was the same.

A sense of distance, of never being able to fit in.

Fear.

The color white—rejected even by darkness.

It became a word to indicate Accelerator, the One-Way Road.

"Be friendly to her? Impossible. It doesn't mean shit. What's the point of giving one yen back to someone you owe a hundred million? That wouldn't even pay the interest on it, so I don't feel like paying it at all. Just thinking about it is fucking stupid. Gives me the creeps—thinking about smiling in the sunlight, all my debts paid."

His voice was awkward.

What am I bragging about my debt for? wondered Accelerator, swearing at himself.

Yomikawa remained silent for a few moments. Then she spoke. "It might not mean anything from me, but you hate yourself for forgetting to pay that debt, don't you? If there was a way to pay back that hundred million, you'd be all over it in a heartbeat. Am I wrong?"

"...Hmph." Accelerator didn't give her a real answer to that.

Yomikawa's tone didn't change, though. She'd been serious from the start. "Like, for example, I never raise a weapon at children. Doesn't matter if they're an esper or whatever, I don't point a weapon at them. That's a rule I set for myself, but..."

"Eh?"

"Why do you think I'm doing that?"

" ... "

"Do you know why I don't want to point weapons at children?"

This bitch..., Accelerator thought to himself. The scent of dark emotions leaking through her voice made him unconsciously think about that scene in the alley.

"There you have it. Maybe the 'quantity' I have can't even be compared. But the 'quality' isn't all that different. So even if we're operating on different scales, it's all in the same category, yeah?" Yomikawa's voice dug into Accelerator. "...It may not look pretty, but all you can do is pay it back, one yen, one coin at a time. Eventually it will pile up and open the way for you. I mean, unlike me, you have the strength. There are plenty of ways for you to repay it all at once."

"That's a funny opinion. You're gonna warp my face, being all wishy-washy like that."

"I guess the easiest way would be to join Judgment. The peace in the city would go up thirty percent just with your name, yeah? I can get the paperwork ready if you want."

"You're insane," Accelerator said in flat refusal.

This power he had wasn't like that. All it let him do was wave his arms and bathe in the blood spatter. The category was lower than nuclear energy, an immensely negative strength with absolutely no way for it to be used for peace. He could do his best, but it would never bring about any results. Through his actions, all he could create was destruction.

But even still.

Maybe he had thought about what-ifs.

If he'd stopped the experiment with his power.

If he could have prevented the Sisters from walking along their road to death.

And...

...if it wasn't too late now.

The dead, which had been scattered before him in the past and might very well be scattered before him again in the future—how much could he reduce that number?

An impractical proposition. One that absolutely couldn't happen.

There was no way he could.

He knew that.

He didn't need someone to tell him that. He'd used this power for so long. He knew it best.

And yet...

"It's bullshit."

"If you just keep accumulating what you're calling bullshit, you'll start paying back that debt."

That is what Aiho Yomikawa said…

…in a voice steeped in sunlight.

INTERLUDE THREE

Hyouka Kazakiri was walking through Academy City.

She was a plain girl. Her waist-length hair color was natural… which sounded nice, but it was simply because she hadn't done anything to it. The only thing, perhaps, was her decision to section off a tuft of hair on the side with an elastic band. Her regular facial features were hidden behind large, unfashionable glasses, and she hadn't a single puff of makeup on. Her school uniform skirt even went down to her knees. It clearly wasn't walking attire for the busy streets.

But her figure drew eyes.

Not for her excellent, pretty looks—the attention was on something more unnatural.

Noise.

The girl, who gave the impression of a small, quietly blooming flower, sometimes became distorted. Like mist blown by wind or a television signal with bad reception, there would be a rasping static as her silhouette grew uncertain before returning to normal. And just when someone saw her summer button-down waver, she was then wearing a blue-colored blazer.

And still, she walked the streets.

The sight would normally cause a big stir, but she received no negative attention in reaction.

Because this was a city of supernatural abilities and scientific technology.

They would accept most unnatural occurrences, not reject them.

However...

"Heeey, who are you?"

An Anti-Skill man came running up to Kazakiri. He was an expert, someone who would even use a firearm if a crime happened and take the initiative to quell it. But his main occupation was that of a teacher. He didn't have the sharpness a real agent would have.

He, too, accepted Kazakiri's presence as part of the city's normal scenery.

His goal wasn't to get rid of her.

But...

"*I swear, making a 3-D image like this...*Where's the esper? This is a pretty elaborate prank."

His eyes weren't looking at Kazakiri.

He had accepted her as part of the cityscape but only as a simple phenomenon.

Supernatural abilities and scientific technology.

Most strange things in this city could be resolved with those words. Academy City—where you could convince yourself of anything if you decided it was created by technology you didn't know about or an experiment.

That was why Hyouka Kazakiri could walk the streets like this.

She could be accepted, not excluded, even though she thought herself a monster, clearly not human in anyone's eyes.

Was that fortunate?

Or was it misfortunate?

Hyouka Kazakiri was a 3-D noise image shaped by the hands of espers. She wouldn't say she was a human with a heart.

She smiled a little.

A slightly bitter, lonely smile.

An all-too-transient expression, which could only be described as human.

"...This is a pretty detailed illusion. Did they think their teacher would start blushing?"

This, too, was accepted.

Save for the most important part.

CHAPTER 4
Gradually Intersecting Pairs
Boy_Meets_Girl (x2).

1

Mikoto Misaka went away somewhere.

He didn't know why, really, but as soon as she'd seen Little Misaka and the tiny one with her, her mood had worsened.

"Hey, wait!" she'd said, her face bright red. "Whose punishment game do you think it is you're here for today?! You weren't going to work your butt off all day for me?!"

Kamijou had responded to her demand honestly. "Huh? You were just after Croaker, weren't you?" he answered.

Then for some reason, Mikoto had nibbled her lip. "...!! What...? Ah, uh, that's right! Now that I have Croaker and Hoppit, I have no more use for you! Who cares about the punishment game?! Idiot!!"

A lance of lightning had flown at him as she shouted, which is why Kamijou was now on the floor in a corner of the underground mall. He'd managed to succeed in repelling her billion-volt attack, but the surprise had made him lose his balance and fall backward.

Wh-what was the problem...?

She'd shouted, "I don't care anymore!!" and run away somewhere at a rapid pace. Kamijou, left behind, wasn't clear on whether she'd released him from his punishment. Now he was loafing around, doing nothing in particular.

What on earth is going on today? he wondered. *What with Little Misaka and Kuroko Shirai...*

The most suspicious of the bunch had to be the girl of about ten with Little Misaka. Her features were exactly the same as Mikoto's—or rather Little Misaka's. Seriously, who was she? He hoped, a bead of cold sweat breaking out on his face, that they hadn't added on another twenty thousand Misakas as a new series or something. It really worried him. In this city, it could actually happen.

With a sigh, he said, "Gah, I'll just ask Little Misaka at some point. I get the feeling I'll be getting a huge invoice later if I let this run its course."

"Why do your shoulders droop with such deep exhaustion? asks Misaka asks Misaka, clinging to your back like a mascot made for soothing the soul."

As the strange, unexpected reply came in response to his muttering, a weight suddenly latched onto his back. The round sensation on it sent a terrible shudder through him, making his hair stand on end.

"Wha— What?! Are you trying to be that tiny old man spirit that crushes you when you give it a piggyback ride?!"

"Misaka's gender is female, and besides, I think talking about occult stuff in Academy City is nonsensical, says Misaka says Misaka, gripping your body tighter to gain a sense of stability. Misaka wants this to be her spot, demands Misaka demands Misaka as an extra."

Fshh. The lukewarm mass of body heat got a tiny bit heavier.

The chilling feeling in his spine reached its climax. "Uwooo-wahh!! What the heck is this?!" he shouted as he reached his hands behind his head, took hold of the thing clinging to his back, and flung it before him like he was slam-dunking it. There, hanging upside down, was the mystery miniaturized Little Misaka.

Who is this kid? he wondered, tilting his head to the side.

The upside-down, mirrored girl followed suit and cocked her own head to the other side.

2

How the hell did it come to this? Accelerator's shoulders drooped.

He was right inside the entrance to the underground mall. Several tables were arranged even outside the stores as open spaces for fast-food joints. Though this was the underground mall, the distinction between a shop's inside and outside was extremely dubious.

At one of those tables was a silver-haired, green-eyed girl wearing a snow-white habit. She was slumped right over the table face-first, buried under a mountain of hamburgers, French fries, salads, and the like. Just for the sake of clarity here—these were all things Accelerator had bought. The girl didn't have a single coin on her.

The trigger for all this happening in the first place was Accelerator's entrance into the mall on his modern-design crutch to search for Last Order, and this mystery girl had, out of nowhere, crashed into him from the side.

With a gait and tone that indicated she was indeed dizzy, she'd said in his direction, "Huh, that's not Touma, not Touma, I thought it was Touma. Why isn't this person Touma? Where did he go? It doesn't matter, I'm so hungry I can't move, all these smells of salt and pepper and meat are making my mouth water, I want to eat that, I want to eat it. What should I do? What do I need to do to eat it?"

"..."

Normally, that would be the moment Accelerator considered smashing her body to bits and leaving it lying around somewhere, but embarrassingly enough, Yomikawa had just been telling him a few minutes ago to do nice things once in a while. He shouldn't have bothered making such strange conversation. There was exactly nothing in his mind telling him he needed to faithfully keep to what she'd told him, but if he punched out the sister in white here and went on, he felt like she'd laugh at him the same way one would at someone who said they quit smoking and didn't last thirty minutes. That would be annoying in its own right.

She kept talking on and on without listening, making him think she resembled the brat somewhat, but he'd rather die before admitting it had caught his attention.

Instead, he kicked the starving sister into a nearby fast-food place and threw his wallet at her. As soon as he'd done that, she'd started spewing absurdities, like wanting to eat this and that and everything on the menu—and that's how they got here.

Accelerator had rented his body out to many projects in the past. He'd thrown plenty more money than he needed into a bank account he didn't use, so this wasn't a financial issue...but still, she'd torn through all those hamburgers, so he had to wonder how big her stomach was.

Incidentally, the nun was holding a small calico cat in her hands, but it didn't seem to be hungry, since it didn't show any interest in the hamburgers. (Then again, it couldn't eat them because of the finely sliced onions.) It was busy mewing and meowing with the stray cats wandering into the mall. Their conversations probably included "We're apparently going to get more flexible muscles this autumn" and "No way?! I've been sharpening my claws this whole time!!" Maybe these cats didn't have any territorial instincts.

Accelerator watched the scene of gluttony. "This is ridiculous...I don't even get this tired dealing with that stupid brat."

"Mgah?"

"Quit stopping so much and just eat everything at once. Besides, isn't there somethin' you wanna say to me?"

"Gulp. Yep. Thanks!"

"...Shit. One word?" Accelerator shook his head a little. This was one handful he'd stumbled across. He prayed for peace in the next world for whichever of her acquaintances had to deal with her on a daily basis.

The nun brought a large bottle of juice to her lips and chugged, following that with enough food to fill a plastic bottle, finishing them in five seconds each.

"Um, so, my name is Index."

"Did you even taste any of it?"

"I was looking for Touma, but then I got hungry. Actually, I think I decided to look for Touma because I was already hungry."

Index tossed the fine ice in the juice bottle into her mouth, and her shoulders trembled a little. Either she was too oblivious or too ravenous to notice the sauce stuck to her face near her mouth. Her shortcomings made her seem just like Last Order.

"…Shit." Accelerator took out a pocket-sized tissue packet and silently threw it at Index's face. She proceeded to engage in a desperate struggle to get the tissues out of the plastic packaging, and he sighed. What was with her seeming lack of modern knowledge?

She's looking for someone, too, eh…?

A suspicious person's face came to mind—one who had been loitering around him, wearing only a blanket, just a little while ago. He flicked on his cell phone, then called up to the screen the facial image data of Last Order (really just her face on a camera shot) and showed it to Index.

"You seen a brat who looks somethin' like this?"

"Nope."

Her answer was swift and decisive.

But it didn't look like she was blowing him off out of lack of interest. She had an odd air of confidence about her.

"I never forget anyone's face, so I'm pretty sure I haven't."

"Eh?" Accelerator frowned, but Index didn't seem to want to explain. Maybe she was fully satisfied from all the hamburgers she ate. With a blissful expression, she slumped down onto the table on her cheek.

"Wow, it was a good thing I ran into you. Really, thank you again. Now I can go look for Touma without worrying about my stomach. Now that I'm full I don't see much of a reason to look for him, but I came all the way here, so I don't think I'll be satisfied until I find him."

"Okay, I see. Well, I'm not helping you."

"It's been a little while since I came here, but I still don't really understand the city, after all. Even though with my brain I'd never forget how the roads go…Maybe just remembering them isn't enough. But whatever the case, I got to meet someone from Academy City."

"Okay, I see. Go ask someone else."

"…What kind of job do you do? Are you busy?"

"Yeah, unfortunately, I'm very busy."

Accelerator put his weight onto his crutch and stood up from his seat.

Alas, by coincidence, he was searching for somebody, too.

3

"So, you're like a host computer controlling all the Little Misakas and stuff?" asked Kamijou, eyes wide.

Last Order (another name that sounded fake, he thought, but stayed quiet about it), having finished her brief explanation, waved her small hands in denial. "Maybe more like a console than a host, corrects Misaka corrects Misaka. The Misakas don't have a centralized body, so there isn't much point in having one piece of the network be a 'core,' says Misaka says Misaka, puffing out her chest and proudly giving a lecture."

Apparently, they'd created her in case a large number of Sisters went out of control and those on the human side had to stop them. A "last order" to allow those outside the Misaka network to intervene.

For someone who sounded so important from all that (though Kamijou honestly didn't feel a sense of reality from it), he wondered what she was dawdling around here for again.

"Um, Misaka came here to thank you for saving us during the experiment, presenting a 'Grateful Crane'–like development."

"Which is what you're telling everyone. What are you really here for?"

"You didn't even believe Misaka for a moment! says Misaka says Misaka, stomping her foot!! Well, Misaka coming to thank you is stretching it since it was a coincidence, says Misaka says Misaka, revealing her true intentions and stuff!"

"Then aren't I right to be suspicious?"

"Your lack of sensitivity gets on Misaka's nerves! says Misaka says Misaka, swinging her arms around and trying to pummel you!"

It seemed like he made her mad. He had no choice. He looked around. "Sorry, sorry, I'm sorry, I'll buy you some popcorn from that place over there, so please forgive me!"

"Do you think you can lead a girl's delicate heart around with mere food?! demands Misaka demands Misaka, getting all shocked and stuff!!"

Wait, huh? It seemed like his method of dealing with Index had sunken quite deeply into his mind. *I shouldn't do that*, he reflected honestly. "Sorry. Then we'll fast."

"Misaka will eat it! Popcorn would be greatly appreciated!! says Misaka says Misaka, showing off a new technique of getting the popcorn but still staying mad!!"

Come on, which is it? Kamijou was getting tired of this, but when Last Order started pulling on his pants, he knew in the end, things would be settled by his food method after all.

He bought a cylindrical tub of popcorn in a sweet caramel flavor and presented it to her. She hugged it to her small body.

"Wow, I think this is the same size as Misaka's head, says Misaka says Misaka, admiring the economy-sized container."

"…Oops. No matter how I look at it, that size is bigger than your stomach."

Of course, a nun he knew would probably devour an entire killer whale without much difficulty. Maybe it wasn't enough to make a fuss about.

Two minutes later…

He discovered the young girl, a giant container of popcorn in one hand and the other over her mouth, crouched over and trembling terribly.

"…You know, you don't have to eat it all."

"Mi…Misaka isn't *stupid* enough to let a gift of food go to waste—*blargh*."

Her previous businesslike tone was completely destroyed now.

Besides, he did sort of think she made a mistake trying to eat all that sweet popcorn without anything to drink.

Hmm. It would be easy if Misaka cheered up this simply, but...

As he wondered about whether he should have gone after her, Last Order came to him, looking for a drink.

He had no choice. Kamijou went and bought her a small plastic bottle of mineral water. After wetting her throat with it, she finally went back to normal.

She spoke. "Misaka stole these, says Misaka says Misaka, bragging about her spoils of war."

"And suddenly you're a bandit? Not bad, Misaka network host... Wait, huh? What are those, goggles? They're the ones Little Misaka and the rest always wear..."

Last Order was pointing her finger at a pair of tough-looking goggles hanging around her neck. They looked like military electronics, like night vision goggles, and seemed very heavy. Maybe these were what Little Misaka was talking about when she mentioned something being stolen from her.

"They don't seem to be made for Misaka to use, so Misaka can't equip them, says Misaka says Misaka, getting a little down in the dumps."

"What? You just need to adjust how long the band is so the goggles fit, right?"

"?"

"Give them to me for a second."

Last Order moved in front of him and stood on her tiptoes, jutting out her chin a bit. This was simply to make it easier for him to take the goggles from around her neck. Finding any deeper significance for her action was something he must not do.

He touched the headgear with a finger and realized it was a band made of rubber. It might be easier to understand by envisioning underwater goggles. A metal fitting was attached at the base of the goggles to adjust the length.

"Sorry, just hold still for a moment," said Kamijou, gripping the goggles themselves. It was easier to pull the band through the fitting this way. He tugged on the thick rubber band and stretched it out.

Then Last Order began to flail. "Ow, ow, ow, ow, ow, ow, says Misaka says Misa—"

"Ah?!" In his surprise, Kamijou let go of the goggles.

The stretched-out rubber band started to go back to its original size...

...and there was a clear *smack* sound on Last Order's face.

"..."

He found it somewhat difficult to go up and talk to Last Order as she rolled around on the floor nearby. As he stood in a fluster, unsure of what to do, the young, teary-eyed girl stood on her tiptoes again, as if to emphasize the goggles around her neck again.

Well, this time I really can't mess it up.

Whenever people think like that, it always happens again.

Smack!! went the noise, which doesn't warrant another explanation.

This time she kicked him over and stomped on him a bunch of times, but after that, she brightened up and offered her goggles to him again.

How admirable.

Kamijou vowed he would take the utmost caution to repay her spirit, finally succeeded in adjusting the rubber band's length, and put the goggles around Last Order's forehead for her. They still looked too big for her, but he managed to get them around her forehead without them sliding.

"Wow!!" cried Misaka, happily putting her hands on the goggles and twirling around.

Come to think of it, Kamijou thought dubiously. *Is she hanging around here by herself? She was with Little Misaka before, but now she's gone. Maybe they got separated.*

He found that hard to believe given that they were in an underground mall, but it was already almost six, and the sun was going down soon. He knew it was best to bring such a dangerous child back to her guardian right away, but was her caretaker around here?

Hmm...If they are nearby, how would I look to them? That's not good. I feel like they'd start yelling stuff like "What are you doing to my kid?"

And then—

At that moment, Kamijou felt eyes on him.

He had a bad feeling about this.

"What's wrong? asks Misaka asks Misaka plainly."

Without answering her innocent voice, he turned around.

Slowly. And fearfully.

When he saw who was there, he moaned.

"It can't be…"

4

"So Touma always, always, *always* leaves me behind and goes off to who knows where. I think it's already a kind of wanderlust. He always goes on journeys before I know it."

"…"

Accelerator, on his modern-design crutch, walked through the underground mall. It was a bit difficult to tell whether it was day or night here. The final train and bus runs were aligned with the last schools to close, so the students walking here and there seemed to have something of an urgency to their steps.

"I wonder what it is. I mean, he doesn't hate the place he's in now, and he doesn't particularly like the places he goes to. Wander, wander, wander, wander, wander—he just wanders off."

"…"

Though he didn't know this Touma person, Accelerator gleaned from her words that he was a terribly annoying guy to be around. For some reason, it irritated him every time she said his name.

Index picked up the calico, who had been hanging around nearby, and asked, "By the way, what are you doing here?"

"Lookin' for someone."

"The person on the *cellulose phone*?"

"So what?" replied Accelerator, not caring.

It wasn't as though he needed to keep it secret. And with this kind of brat, trying to hide it would just make her ask over and over and over again. That would be annoying. He knew someone a little like her, so he was already familiar with that behavior.

Index picked up the cat, tilting her head. "Hey, by the way, I didn't thank you yet."

"Shut up and go home, stupid brat. Pretty sure bothering with someone like you's just gonna make this take way longer than it needs to."

"I didn't thank you yet."

"…"

She pretended he hadn't said anything.

Accelerator shot her an irked look, but she didn't care. "That girl from before, right? I can help you look for her until I find Touma if you want," she said with a smile.

Without knowing anything about the person she was talking to.

"…Bullshit," he muttered unintentionally in reply to her perfectly innocent words.

Today was when he learned how tiring it could be to go along with other people's kindness.

5

There he found Blue Hair and Motoharu Tsuchimikado.

Both looked once at Kamijou's face, then at Last Order's, then back up at Kamijou's.

Then they both spoke at the same time.

""You little bugger!!""

"I don't even understand what that reaction means!!" Kamijou shouted. Right next to him, Last Order had already grown cautious as she edged behind him.

Tsuchimikado and Blue Hair didn't care.

"Nyaa! Well, I mean with Ms. Komoe there's at least her real age and other stuff involved, but what is this, nyaa? How are you going to explain yourself, nyaa?!"

"Y-you bastard!! I know you have no principles, but there's a limit, dumbass!! How far will you go to set yourself up with no blind spots?! I bet you'll start chattin' up a cute old lady on a balcony hunched over a cat on her lap!"

""However!"" said Blue Hair and Tsuchimikado at the same time, glaring at Kamijou.

Then they smiled as wide as they could.

""As your friends! We'll pray for your success!!""

Deciding the clearly slanderous duo needed to be removed, Kamijou clenched his fist. "You..."

Imagine Breaker. A good name. I'll teach you—this is exactly the time I should be using it.

Bam bam bam bam bam!! As a brawl erupted among the three, Last Order timidly spoke up.

"U-um, are those your friends? asks Misaka asks Misaka, trying to understand the situation."

"Children mustn't watch this! Their lifestyles and idiotic conversations are still too stimulating for little kids!!"

Kamijou swung his fist, meaning to stamp a big R rating on the idiots' foreheads. Peaceful days seemed distant as of yet.

6

Mikoto folded her arms, offended, as she hurried through the mall.

Even now, the Tokiwadai Middle School uniform seemed to stick out like a sore thumb. Students walking by would glance over at her. She never minded it at all, but today, her patience was running strangely thin.

You're the one who promised you'd do this punishment game, you idiot..., she muttered internally.

Just the fact that she was angry about something like this made her even less happy. However she felt about it, she couldn't accept how it weighed so heavily in her thoughts.

Even after leaving the place (or rather, the boy), Mikoto had been throwing brief glances over her shoulder. As she did, there was one thing above all others that made her unable to deal with the situation calmly.

...He had the gall to be relieved.

Slam. She'd softly stomped on the mall floor before realizing it.

A sigh came out.

Well, he would. It was just a regular punishment game. He's the one who suggested it in the first place. How could he forget? Still, I was dragging him all over against his will. I guess it's only natural he'd want to end it as soon as he could. But...

If this was how it was going to be, she was a complete fool for having a good time by herself.

Her eyes fell to the small paper bag from the cell phone company, peering into it at the visible tiny frog mascot, thinking, *It's only natural, but...*

For some reason, she *really* felt like she'd been left behind.

She saw her face reflected in a sparkly clean support beam, her mouth twisted into a pouty look. Seeing that made her want to slap herself across the face.

*It isn't like what that idiot did goes against the rules of the punishment game or anything. And **that girl** being with him isn't a problem, either. So what the heck am I doing?*

Now that she thought about it calmly, maybe she was acting pretty immature.

Who cared about some shitty punishment game?

If it was going to make her feel like this anyway, she shouldn't have made the bet during the Daihasei Festival at all. For one reason or another, it felt like things had been lost because of that game. For Mikoto herself and for the people nearby.

She kind of wanted to curl up in the corner of her room and hide.

She sort of felt like doing something about this stress that had nowhere to go right now.

Wasn't there anything she could do?

" ... "

Looking around, she only saw an arcade in terms of places for entertainment. There was a game called Skill Attack sitting in front, infamous for having an extremely high difficulty level. Basically, it was a repurposed ability measurement device. One would blast their ability into the baseball mitt–shaped shock-resistant "target," and it would give them a number representing the strength of the attack. It was just a stress-relieving machine.

Mikoto wandered over that way. The moment the pastry shop next to the arcade went out of view, anyone could tell just how frayed her nerves were.

There was nothing "proper young lady–like" about her right now.

She put several hundred-yen coins into the machine.

The "target" in question was designed like a signboard. It was a square baseball mitt that looked like it was made of urethane, attached to a supporting metal pipe. Compared to the actual machine, the target was oddly shiny, so it was probably disposable. Maybe they changed it every other day.

It's probably not set up to handle Level Fives anyway.

She sighed.

Most machines like this could only handle up to Level Four espers, and even if its slogan mentioned the level, it was generally good manners to stop it at Level Three.

Jeez. I even have to take it easy when venting stress..., she complained to herself.

Then a small warning label caught her eye.

This is what it said:

"The latest version assumes ability usage. We are collecting data now in order to allow Level Five users. Your cooperation is appreciated!"

Mikoto froze.

Then the stress within her began to bubble out as a smirk formed on her face.

Eerie crackling noises came from her rustling bangs.

Silently, she took a deep, deep breath.

And she decided to cooperate.

With everything.

"That freaking idiot!! How dare you! Break a promise! You made!!

And here I was…putting in so much effort to check all the score listings during the festival!!"

Crackle, bang, snap, bang, crack!! came the thunderous sounds as the ability-measurement-device game machine rattled around in every direction. It probably had *some* shock-resistant features, but it bowed before force enough to tear the machine from the earthquake-resistant supports connecting it to the floor. Low, dull buzzing noises started going off nearby. The relaxed mall atmosphere made a one-eighty as the students nearby panicked and tried to flee, saying things like "Ugyah!" and "Wh-what's that?!" and "Wait, wait a second!!"

Having beaten the hell out of the machine, Mikoto was breathing loudly, her shoulders bobbing up and down.

Ding-ding! ♪ came a soft electronic tone.

She looked. Apparently, she'd set a new high score.

"…I feel empty," she said suddenly. "…"

In the end, she decided to leave the big machine and go back the way she came.

There was no point getting riled up by herself. She decided to admit she was being immature and apologize. It wasn't like one of the Sisters getting a present was some kind of mistake. She was incredibly uncertain the idiot would simply let her say sorry, but she wanted to try doing the adult thing this time. She took a deep breath.

But there was still the punishment game.

It was vexing that he thought she'd let the war spoils from the Daihasei Festival she put so much effort into wresting away just end like that.

Whatever the case, she had to find him again and talk to him. She sped up her pace.

7

After finally managing to coerce Blue Hair and Motoharu Tsuchimikado to reflect on their actions, Kamijou checked the digital clock on his cell phone. It was already past six. Outside, on the surface, the sun had probably set and let the night in.

"Hmm. Your acquaintances are very unique, says Misaka says Misaka, folding her arms and tilting her head. And I wonder why I still feel somewhat sick to my stomach, says Misaka says Misaka, rechecking each of the terms she heard."

That's what Last Order said, but Kamijou estimated it wouldn't be too much of a problem. If she didn't understand, then great.

"Ack, it's already this late? says Misaka says Misaka, panicking a little bit," she said all of a sudden.

As far as he could see, no clocks were hanging on the walls, and one couldn't see the sky from the underground mall. Maybe she got some kind of information over the rumored Misaka network.

She twirled back around to face him. "Um, Misaka has to go home soon, says Misaka says Misaka, hating to be the bearer of bad news."

"Well, it is getting late." Kamijou was just thinking it was time for little kids to get home anyway, so he felt reassured.

"Yep," she said with a little nod. "I wanted to stay with you longer, though, says Misaka says Misaka, getting all down in the dumps and stuff. We met here by coincidence, but Misaka meant it when she said she wanted to thank you, says Misaka says Misaka, speaking her mind."

Last Order put her hands on the goggles on her forehead.

"And I got these, too," she said. "But I think *he'll* be worried, says Misaka says Misaka, remembering and continuing. If it gets too late, he might go out to look for Misaka this time, and Misaka doesn't want to cause him trouble, says Misaka says Misaka with a smile."

"I see," said Kamijou offhandedly. He didn't know who she meant, but he got the vague impression he was a sort of good guy.

"He's weak," continued Last Order. "He got hurt a lot and could never protect what he had, and the hands he used to save them are all messed up now, says Misaka says Misaka, trying to convey fragments of information. Misaka doesn't want to put any more of a burden on him, so this time it's Misaka's turn to protect him, reveals Misaka reveals Misaka."

"Oh." He only understood maybe half of what she was saying, but he nodded anyway. Her words were free of any lies. He wasn't a sort of good guy—he was *definitely* a good guy.

"He's cool sometimes, too, adds Misaka adds Misaka. Even if he gets all bloody and messed up, he still fights for Misaka, boasts Misaka boasts Misaka."

Huh. I get this really strong sense of familiarity about that guy's behavior. He didn't have any grounds for saying that, so he kept his mouth shut.

Kamijou watched for a few moments as Last Order ran away, waving and saying "bye-bye" to him. He guessed it was getting close to the time schools would normally close—in other words, the last trains and buses—because suddenly the crowds in the underground mall were moving urgently. Her small body slipped through them and was out of sight before he knew it.

Welp, time to go, he thought, turning on his heel, suddenly catching sight of someone he knew.

"Hmm?"

She started coming toward him.

8

"Oh, it's Touma…"

Next to him, Index stopped dead in her tracks. She was looking down the passageway.

"The guy you were lookin' for?"

"Yep."

Accelerator randomly looked over in that direction, but in the crowd, he couldn't discern who she was looking at. Besides, in this situation, he wouldn't even know who she was referring to anyway.

Index stared at Accelerator.

He said, "Go."

"But what about your acquaintance?"

"Don't worry," he spat. "Just found her."

The direction he indicated was the same way Index had looked—directly in front of them. He saw a small girl making her way through the mainly middle school student crowd and running toward him.

Accelerator knew her name.

He didn't know if it was her real name or how much value was contained within a name created by scientists as a convenience for paperwork. But that was true for Accelerator, too. There was probably nobody who knew his real name.

Whatever it was, if she only had one name to go by, then it was the one that referred to her.

So Accelerator spoke.

"Last Order!"

Hearing her name, the small girl put even more energy into her steps. An idiotic expression of happiness was plastered to her face.

Next to Accelerator, as he watched, he heard small pattering footsteps.

All Index said was, "Okay, then bye. Thanks!" Then, "Touma!!"

There was a pep in her light steps. The girl who had only been with him for a few minutes left his side and ran beyond the crowds of people.

She didn't turn back.

Neither did Last Order.

The two girls met at one point in the underground mall, passed by each other, and left, neither noticing.

Each running toward the place she needed to be.

It didn't even take ten seconds for Last Order to fly up to Accelerator.

"I'm back, says Misaka says Misaka, giving the proper greeting... *Ow!* Why do you keep karate chopping me like that?! cries Misaka cries Misaka in a fake way, holding her head."

He hit the girl's head relentlessly, taking out his discontentedness on her. "What the hell have you been doing this whole time?"

"Getting people to play with Misaka, says Misaka says Misaka, answering honestly."

"Hmph," snorted Accelerator.

He glanced back again, wondering what became of the terribly annoying sister.

But from here, he couldn't discern anything.

All he saw was an indistinct crowd of people.

Just like always.

INTERLUDE FOUR

The Facility for the Miniature Reproduction and Administration of Phenomena.

That was the name of the building in which Sasha Kreutzev sat.

More specifically, it was a cluster of buildings built by the Russian Catholic Church. The organization mainly analyzed and resolved spiritual phenomena, but when such incidents occurred, they would build an actual-size facility that was exactly like the phenomenon.

Their exhaustive accuracy could best be described as "merciless."

In the Crossist faith dogma, the souls of the dead went to either heaven, purgatory, or hell. Therefore, there was no such thing as a soul that stayed in this world—at least, that was the story. Hence, the Russian Catholic Church considered all on earth who claimed to be dead to be "fakes taking advantage of death's sorrow." They sometimes defined such things like missing pieces of a jigsaw puzzle—they had an effect by going away.

But there were very rare cases, such as jack-o'-lantern, whose souls (actually) wandered around after death. Such cases, though, were judged by Crossism to be the souls of sinners "without the right to go to Heaven, whilst also barred from Hell."

All those who claimed to be dead, without exception, were mortal.

That was the singular end point of their conclusions.

Whether real or fake, they were the enemy. The Russian Catholic

Church handled such troublesome folks by "rounding them up and purging them all at once." It didn't matter if ghosts had regrets, or reminisced about their life, or tried to scare people out of spite. If they were wandering on earth, they were evil. The Church's style was to laugh away the trivial circumstances of any sort and crush them.

Stories of exceptions existed, of course, such as people resurrected by the Son of God and the twelve apostles. Those were acts only capable by such preeminently historic figures like the Son of God and saints, though. Some random sinner or begrudging corpse could never do that.

They had a facility where they received search information so they could "defeat the *enemy*, no questions asked."

That place was here.

It gave the impression of a city built in the middle of the desert for Hollywood filming purposes, but their giant papier-mâché film props couldn't hold a candle to the precision of the ones here.

Also, there had originally only been one or two props, but because of all the "research props" they'd built around the facility, it had grown to the size of a city that could fit two or three whole towns inside. It could be said this was a method only Russia could use, given the vast lands it possessed, cutting straight across the continent of Eurasia.

Sasha put a few drops of brandy in her tea and drank from her cup with a book in one hand inside a building modeled perfectly after a certain palace. Facility for the Miniature Reproduction and Administration of Phenomena was a painfully long name. Even within the facility, within this movie-like town, this building was the old-timer "reference prop" of the bunch.

The palace held a mixture of civilizations inside, and though it was the foundation of Crossist occultism, various objets d'art were mounted up in the top of the roof, ballooning outward like an onion.

"..."

Unbefitting Sasha's slight frame, she drip-dropped more brandy into her tea like a lover of sweets pouring sugar in. The brandy wasn't for flavor—this was a tea-flavored alcoholic drink.

The thick book in her hand had the title *Actual Images of Angels as Variants* printed on the cover. Its "original copy" would have been in the *real* palace, but this book was a prop belonging to this facility, perfectly re-created down to the letter. Even though it wasn't a library of grimoires, the facility was renowned for how many "manuscripts" it contained.

"*...A precaution regarding angels being called down into human bodies.*"

Sasha's hand stopped on the page she was looking for.

Her slender fingers traced the handwritten letters, which had been inscribed before the printing press was invented. At times, she frowned at the unfamiliar decryption method, but she didn't rest. There was a reason she persisted in the work she wasn't used to.

Something strange had happened to her body.

Visibly speaking, she now had a slight, irregular tremble in her fingers. *In*visibly speaking, she now had a strange ability to sense mana...though it was actually closer to a biological rejection. It depended on how much mana there was, but when a large amount of it was used close to her, she could feel a sort of pressure in her chest.

She'd been feeling it since the end of August, but Sasha herself had no idea what had happened. After getting looked at in a large-scale facility, it was similar to the state one would be in if dense concentrations of Telesma—angelic power—were residing in her body for a long period of time. She'd never done any sorcery experiments like that.

What on earth had happened to her body?

Figuring it out wasn't just Sasha's job anymore. The entire Russian Catholic Church had already transformed it into a pending issue, acknowledged behind the scenes. Telesma was something everyone in Crossism borrowed, and it wasn't rare for it to directly reside within someone's body. Even Sasha used it in battle. But this was the first time her unique "symptoms" had appeared.

The entirety of Russian Catholicism, to speak nothing of the group within that framework she belonged to, Annihilatus—the so-called "white paper annihilators"—was now paying close attention to this incident regarding her. That made her worried, too. She had a guess that something was going on, but for now, her own body came first.

"The most major instance in this world of Telesma residing in a human was, of course, the Annunciation. When all the Telesma of the Son of God, immense enough to support and guide this entire world, enters the womb, it normally and without a doubt causes death by explosion. However, the Holy Virgin Mother, by maximizing her own attribute as the heavenly Father's partner..."

Sasha didn't realize something—she was nodding along as she followed the letters on the page.

Then the devil's hands, approaching her from behind.

"Sashenka~. ♪"

The frightfully silky voice caused her expressionless features to jump in surprise all at once.

But she was already too late.

Two hands burst forth under Sasha's arms, squeezing hold of her small chest before she could put herself on alert.

A voice behind her spoke. "You know, I think it's time for little hardworking Sashenka, absorbed in her book and not watching her surroundings, to take a break, okay? Yes—*nuwooahh*?!"

The latter part turned into a scream as Sasha took a hammer and an L-shaped nail puller from her belt and immediately prepared for battle. Whether by some mechanism or sorcery, the hammer's hitting surface only needed to touch the table to slam a huge crater in it and make it explode.

Sasha Kreutzev turned around, weapons in hand.

The person behind her blanched. "S-Sashenka? We're in a facility for perfectly reproducing spiritual phenomena, and if you go around breaking things so easily, it makes it hard for the facility to do its job...!!"

"Answer one. Please send any written letters of apology to Bishop Nikolai Tolstoj."

"Wait, you'd be the one writing that, Sashenka! Hell, why does Sashenka look so lovely when she's playing innocent?!"

Flap, flap, flap, flap, flap!! She waved her arms desperately around. Sasha sighed.

The woman was Sasha's direct superior.

Her name was Vasilisa. The signs of aging had begun to show in her fair skin, and she was extremely conscious of things like ultraviolet rays and skin blemishes. Standard battles with the Unhallowed, or "those who should not exist," were conducted at night, but lately she'd picked up a bad habit where she'd say, "Staying up late is bad for my skin" and go home by herself. Sasha quite frequently caught her body in a lasso and flung her right into the middle of the "herd of targets."

But she was still Vasilisa.

Why she insisted on the name of a heroine from Russian folklore Sasha didn't know, but it was obviously fake. Vasilisa was just barely leaving her twenties, but nobody knew her exact age. She'd said, "Women are better with lots of mysteries!" a few times—but when Sasha said it more importantly meant nobody would celebrate her birthday, she was depressed for half the day.

Sasha's incredibly immature superior was driving her up a wall. Not in the past tense, but in the present continuous tense. That was important.

Vasilisa trailed the page Sasha had been reading. "Reading something old and dusty again? Does that mean you haven't figured out what went wrong with your body, Sashenka? In that case, I'd be happy to give you a thorough checkup, heh-heh-heh-ah-ha…"

Sasha took the hammer she was twirling in her hand and brought it down on the crown of Vasilisa's head. She heard a dull *bang!!* "Question one. Do you prefer hammers or screwdrivers?"

"You already hit me with it, so that's not a very good question. You've got so much nonsensical destructive force in you as usual."

Sasha didn't want to hear that from the person who never batted an eyelash at the magical torture hammer slamming into her. She liked to joke around, but she was probably stronger than Sasha.

"By the way, that Telesma in you—it's Gabriel's, right?"

"Question two. What about it?"

"That's normally impossible, isn't it? That would mean it's more than the twelve apostles, right?"

"Question three. What—?"

"Bzzt! The POWER OF GOD was the angel chosen for the Annunciation. And if more power than the twelve apostles got shut away in a woman's body, then…My, oh my! Sashenka, could you be…? Does your belly look any bigger—? *Bgghoh*?!"

Sasha swung her saw right into Vasilisa's smiling face.

Not a scratch on her.

"Oops, sorry, I didn't mean it. After all, Sashenka, you wear that hard-core bondage outfit all the time. You couldn't stand making a baby with no pleasure, could you?"

"Question four. Do not foul even a single page of the sacred New Testament, you complete jerk. As an additional explanation, this straitjacket is something you forced me to wear by abusing your authority, remember?"

The so-called "bondage outfit" Sasha was wearing consisted of a red mantle, under which she wore a suit that was basically just very revealing underwear, along with a black belt. It was the kind old perverts might show up wearing on the street at night. Vasilisa claimed, "If it looks like an Unhallowed will possess your body, as a last-ditch option, you can bind yourself!" but no matter how she looked at it, she was just into this stuff.

Sasha, for her part, would rather not have even touched such a sluttish straitjacket. Unfortunately, Vasilisa was her direct superior, and she had to uphold her written oath. It would be absurd if rebelling over something she couldn't do anything about landed her in a convent (read: *guardhouse*).

Not all Russian Catholic sisters dressed like this, of course. It wasn't a circus of perverts.

Hiding herself behind her red mantle again, Sasha glared at her superior.

Vasilisa, clad in a perfectly honest red habit, cackled. "What? You hate it that much?"

"Answer two. That question itself is an insult to my personality."

"Then let's change your outfit," she said simply.

"...?"

Sasha looked at her superior through her pestiferous bangs, only a little taken aback.

Vasilisa began to fish through her old-fashioned bag she'd set on the floor at her feet. "Well, you see, lately I've been looking into a bunch of stuff about Academy City and the occultism of island nations for business..."

"..."

She didn't like where this was headed.

She felt like she shouldn't look inside the bag.

They weren't borrowing the aid of an astrological facility—but for some reason, a rather cold premonition was insistently poking at her mind.

"And get this—there's a unique culture within Academy City. Of course, when I say *culture*, you know what I mean. Japan really is a good reference for countries. Well, I got my hands on some serious stuff, so I motivated myself to sew one of these, right down to the stitching!"

Sasha looked at the door, but before she could get very far estimating how thick and durable it was...

"Sashenkaaa, have you ever heard of Magical Powered Kanamin?"

She used her L-shaped nail puller to bust down the heavy door and flee.

One look at the "clothing" Vasilisa was unfurling for her with a full smile and she nearly let herself start crying. She knew Vasilisa had been collecting pieces of Japan's suspicious otaku culture through France, but she hadn't considered the woman's tastes to be that ridiculous.

Anything but that glittering, shiny outfit.

Sasha Kreutzev was a combat nun belonging to the Russian Catholic Church's special unit Annihilatus. Their battles were cruel ones, their goals the utter destruction of "all who should not exist" in this world. There was no good reason for running around a battlefield in such fluttery, thin clothing.

Maybe she should transfer to another department.

Nobody would want to die in battle wearing something so hard-core.

CHAPTER 5

A Sunset Spent in Vagueness

Hard_Way, Hard_Luck.

1

"Wow, it's raining, says Misaka says Misaka, looking up at the night sky, a little bummed out she can't see the moon."

On the now-dark streets, Last Order was catching raindrops in her palms.

In Academy City, once the last schools let out, the trains and buses stopped as well. Most residents were out of sight. The only ones left were the gutsy types who stayed out late, deciding they didn't need to go home today. The nearby bus stop, simple with a galvanized iron roof, was empty, too.

The rain continued to patter.

It wasn't enough to warrant an umbrella, but those gutsy students were nowhere to be seen on the streets, either. They'd probably decided not to stand around on the roads, talking and causing a ruckus inside stores instead.

As Last Order wandered all over the place, excited, Accelerator glared at her, tired of it. "You're being annoying. Go stay put over there or something."

"Oh, is that the puppy who's been hanging about near here in that bus stop taking shelter from the rain?! says Misaka says Misaka, darting off and beginning her pursuit...*Urk!!*"

"Do you need a collar and a leash or what, you stupid brat?!"

He grabbed the back of the small girl's head and kept her in place. If she ran away again, he wouldn't have the energy to go after her this time. A nearby building could find itself destroyed after he finished venting.

Last Order flapped her arms around. "Misaka thinks she'll be okay without you being so overprotective, says Misaka says Misaka, requesting freedom and release."

"Save your stupid frontier spirit for your dreams. Anyway, I'm not being protective, and if you cause me any more trouble, I'm gonna punch you in the stomach and knock you out. It'll probably be easier that way."

"There you go again—you don't have to be so shy about it, says Misaka says Misaka, pointing at you crossly...Why are you making such a tight fist? asks Misaka asks Misaka with a bright smile meant to calm your anger and stuff."

What a pain, he said to himself with a sigh.

Not everything in a tailored daily life was bright. People would always be unhappy with *something*, no matter what the world was like. An ultimate world where everything was best for one—when a person thought about it, that just meant a space where they could be self-righteous and completely ignore the needs of others.

The languid annoyance he felt was like a contract price for living in the world.

He knew that.

Accelerator smiled sardonically at himself.

How terrifying it was to grow used to something.

Who did he think he was, accepting everything around him as natural, even *complaining* about things?

When he'd already done all that.

He should be thanking God or whoever was above the clouds just that he was standing here now.

As he walked, deep in reflection, a voice reached his ears.

"Ow!! ...Misaka fell down, says Misaka says Misaka, giving a situation report from the ground."

"Quit complaining about nothing."

"Misaka scraped herself, says Misaka says Misaka, looking carefully at her hands."

Last Order got up off the rain-soaked road. She had a little mud on her, and her hands, wet with moisture from the ground, had tiny scrapes on them. A red color began slowly seeping into them.

"Misaka thinks she needs disinfectant, says Misaka says Misaka, getting a little teary-eyed."

"Spit on it or something."

"Misaka thinks she needs disinfectant!! shouts Misaka shouts Misaka again, sounding like she's about to start bawling!!"

"...You're one annoying pest, you know that? Just forget it. Let's get back to Yomikawa's place."

"..." Last Order fell silent.

Accelerator looked over. She bit her small lip and said abruptly, "All right, says Misaka says Misaka, convinced. It hurts, but Misaka will get through it, says Misaka says Misaka, plodding after you."

As though trying to do what he said, she kept her eyes forward, not sparing any more glances at the scrapes on her palms.

But it seemed like she was just forcing herself not to look at them.

Her small mouth clammed up, and she walked after Accelerator without a word. Not speaking put an odd pressure on him. It seemed to him like she was a moment away from crying.

"...Bullshit," he said, accompanied by teeth sucking.

If she got noisy, that would be annoying, too. Accelerator used the hand not on his modern crutch to push Last Order away by her forehead with his index finger. He didn't put much force into it, but the suddenness made her start to fall backward.

"Wah! says Misaka says Misa—?!"

She flapped her arms about, but in the end, she couldn't regain her balance and fell onto her backside.

Not onto any hard asphalt.

She fell onto the bench of the roofed bus stop.

Startled, Last Order looked about the bus stop, protected by its galvanized iron roof.

Accelerator spoke without looking at her. "Wait there. If you move, I'll beat you to a pulp."

He spat on the road.

After a bitter click of his tongue, he walked toward a pharmacy, supported by his crutch. It was only two hundred meters away, but it was incredibly annoying to him to have to walk that far.

He went in.

It was far too big for a pharmacy. All sorts of shelves sat all over the place; just those made it feel oppressive. Still, the ceiling was five times the shelves' height, which relieved the sensation somewhat.

The last school closing time had passed, and there weren't many customers.

Because of what pharmacies were for, they had to be open at all hours. The store clerk in front of him, though, had "I want to close up and watch TV" written all over his face.

Antiseptic solution and bandages..., he thought at first, but decided instead on smaller adhesive bandages. They were really small scrapes. They didn't need an entire roll of bandages.

"Overprotective..."

He made a face, remembering the impudent line.

And now he was having a staring contest with a box of adhesive bandages, shopping basket hanging from one arm and his face anxious. This was nuts. A screw must have popped loose somewhere in him. Angrily, he threw a package of adhesive bandages into his basket and headed up to the register on his crutch.

When he opened his wallet, he saw only pocket change left there.

He had to think for a few moments before remembering how the strange nun calling herself Index had vanished with his food expenses.

"...Piece of shit," he muttered to himself, causing the person behind the register to almost jump out of his skin. He probably didn't know who Accelerator really was, but the aura he felt emanating from him was too dangerous.

Then, on a shelf fixed to the counter next to the register, he spotted more colorful varieties of adhesive bandages. They looked like they were meant for children. The store seemed to have a surplus after stocking things for the Daihasei Festival—some simple first aid kits could be seen as well on shelves.

"What's this? Is it different from normal?" he asked.

He could almost see the person behind the register's heart leap into his throat as he desperately answered. According to him, they all had some kind of childlike modification, indeed, like antiseptic that wouldn't seep into the wound, or adhesive plaster that wouldn't stick, or fragrant bandages that covered the scent of medicine.

Meant for children. Accelerator thought for a moment. *Overprotective.*

Bang!! He kicked the counter with one foot.

The employee looked about to faint from fright. Nevertheless, when Accelerator tossed "for children" antiseptic and adhesive bandages into his basket, the employee's face softened a little. Maybe he thought he was a kid who hated scabs, despite his appearance.

Accelerator managed to fish out enough coins to pay for them.

The trains were done for the day anyway, so he wouldn't need to leave money in his wallet for anything.

He left the store and walked out into the street. It had started to drizzle. He lifted his pharmacy bag up toward the streetlight and saw a deformed mascot character on it, smiling at him.

"...Fuckin' stupid," he spat.

Yomikawa had asked him if he wasn't used to doing things like this. What kind of question was that? He'd never get used to it. What the hell was this, anyway? Wasn't he just about the furthest away from this stuff possible before? He'd beaten over ten thousand people to death, and here he was, zealously hurrying down the street at night with a bag of adhesive bandages for a couple of tiny scrapes. It was crazy. He'd gone mad. Anyone seeing this would have been confused, too. What other reaction could they have but to sneer at him?

Was it okay to get used to this?

Was it okay to worry about one tiny little injury?

Was it okay for a monster to do it, when he'd spilled at least ten thousand liters of blood?

"Bullshit," he cursed.

He'd given an answer to that on August 31. He could be the biggest pile of trash ever, but that had nothing to do with the brat next to him. In cases where that brat could be hurt, and only then, he'd be decent and do something about it, no matter how out of place it seemed.

It was a good perspective.

But it wasn't enough by itself.

Another way to look at it was that he was pushing his burdens onto the brat.

Wasn't he just redirecting the responsibility for motivating him?

What the hell am I looking for...? he thought, lightly gritting his teeth. *What am I all angry for? What do I feel like I'm missing? Hah, I'm further behind than I thought. You should know best—this whole "finding myself" thing just isn't me.*

Then his thoughts cut off.

Thud!!

A black minivan speeding down the road had crashed into him.

It was a single attack from behind.

The place he was standing was a sidewalk, separate from the roadway.

A thick guardrail blocked the roadway from the sidewalk.

However.

It didn't take much for the jet-black minivan to smash through onto the sidewalk Accelerator was on. The driver didn't seem to have hit the brakes, either. The impact flung pieces of the automobile, like its headlights and bumper, all over, and there was the sound of a beam smashing against the shattered front windshield. Iron plates from the torn-apart guardrail flew into the air, slamming into shutters belonging to business buildings facing the road. One thunderous roar gave way to another.

The street corner looked like a bomb had hit it.

And in the midst of it all...

Accelerator was standing there calmly, the same way he had been three seconds ago.

His hand was on the side of his neck.

He cracked it loudly.

His thin fingers were touching the electrode choker—the on/off switch.

His "reflection" was active.

Academy City's strongest Level Five, who wouldn't be scratched even from a direct hit by a nuclear weapon, now reigned.

The hell...? He turned around.

He stared at the black minivan that had charged him.

The iron plates all around it had been cratered like they'd been hit by a cannonball. In the middle was lodged something he wasn't sure what to call—a car or wreckage—flattened to a pulp.

The sun had already set, yet its front headlights were off. They hadn't broken when the minivan hit. They'd been switched off to begin with.

Almost like they didn't want me to know they were sneaking up on me, eh?

Plus, he spotted traces of someone forcing off the license plate and replacing it. Despite the impact being enough to shatter the windshield, it didn't look like the airbags had activated; the thing seemed to be a stolen vehicle to begin with, given the wrenched-open lock on the door.

Which means it's, well, the usual.

In the driver's seat, which was smashed beyond all recognition, a man dressed in black was moaning.

Special forces–esque armored clothing and a black mask covering his head. The man was thorough in his concealment, even wearing thick ski goggles to perfectly hide his eyes.

...Either he's got somethin' against me, or a research group is out to try to use me for their own purposes.

A smile split across Accelerator's face.

He smiled, delighted, at the military pistol grip holstered near the driver's chest.

So they came. I knew idiots like you would come. Shitheads **tryin'**
to bring me back. *Walking garbage cans who can't tell their asses*
from their elbows.

Accelerator looked upward.

He looked up at the driver's face, slightly higher than his, and
smiled.

"—I'll fucking kill you."

Bam!! A huge roar echoed through the night city.

It happened in an instant.

Accelerator jumped toward the driver's seat through the windshield-
less window. His slender arms, as though sucked in, drew near the
man in black's face. More specifically, his mouth. Four fingers, from
his index finger to his pinkie, drove into the man's mouth. His pale
hand tore through his black knife-proof mask, driving deep into
his throat. With his leftover thumb, he held up the man's jaw from
below.

Then he pulled his hand back.

Grrrk—the sound of his jaw dislocating.

"Ah-ha-ha-gya-hah-ah-ha-ha-ha-hi-hi-hi-gya-ha-hah-hah-
hah-ah-ha-ha-ha-ha-ha!!"

A laugh exploded out of Accelerator as he dragged the man's body
out of the driver's seat like a fisherman reeling in a tuna, then flung
him away behind him. He flew over the sidewalk and crashed into a
building shutter.

Smash!! came the noise, booming like thunder.

He heard a high-pitched squealing gasp come from the backseat
of the black minivan.

There were more.

Accelerator's red eyes squirmed and writhed.

"Hmmm? This is fun. Ah-ha-ha. Holy shit, this is amazing, this is
insane, you shithead!!"

He dove like a wild animal through the front window.

He tore up the passenger seat like wild grass, then stepped into the backseat. *Bgrbghee!!* The entire vehicle vibrated strangely. Almost like the metal and interior of the van were trying to avoid him of their own accord. Its frame was already twisted, and he heard a succession of bolts bouncing out of their sockets and window panes breaking. As though the vehicle were a hot-air balloon made of metal, trying to expand.

Another man was in the rear seat.

Before the man in black could draw his gun in his haste, Accelerator grabbed his head and slammed it straight down. *Gonk!!* came the dull sound as the seat split open to let the man's head sink into its cotton insides.

Only the sound of short, muffled breathing came through.

"Ha-ha-ha…Ah, now I'm bored, goddamn it. I'm over this. I ain't a demon."

Accelerator grinned.

"Shit. I won't kill ya. That'd be a pain. If you act now, I'll let you off with a fifty percent discount."

"Ah, ah…" The man's voice was unclear, his mouth buried in the seat as it was. Even so, he barely managed to croak out words. "…Ah…fifty…you mean…money…?"

"Nope."

Accelerator slowly shook his head.

"I'll only tear off fifty percent of your skin. If you're still alive, you're off the hook."

There was an insect-like screech.

Accelerator smiled.

With joy, with happiness, with bliss, with amusement, like licking an ice cream cone after coming off a diet.

Then.

Grsshhh!! came a scraping from the road surface as three black minivans ground to a halt surrounding Accelerator. He looked out the broken windows at them. These vehicles were probably stolen, too, but he sighed—must've been a lot of work to find more of the same exact kind.

"I'm bored."

In any case, he'd have to cancel the special 50 percent–off deal for now.

Accelerator grabbed the man's insect-like face with all five fingers like a basketball.

There was a rush of air as though he'd swung a metal bat. He roughly tossed the man in black away through a glassless window.

The defeated skidded across the asphalt. Without bothering to watch the comedy, the three surrounding minivans' back doors slid open with a clatter.

But nobody got out.

There was only an endless array of gun muzzles on presentation.

Accelerator sighed at the sight, at the same time driving his fist straight down as if to vent his frustration. His vector-controlled strike dealt fatal damage to the vehicle's frame, which was already twisted and broken. All its pipes began to crack apart, and sparks flew into them.

Bang!! came the explosive wind and heat, spreading in every direction, swallowing up all their surroundings.

He heard a series of muffled screams from the three minivans. Sure, they were inside, wearing masks over their faces, but an extremely hot wind mass had just struck them from point-blank range. Several, burned in their throats, writhed in pain, and a few even ended up rolling out of the opened sliding doors in the back of the vehicles.

"Fantastic play, guys," came the voice from the flames. "I'll make sure you look good dying. You're welcome."

Accelerator casually walked into the flames and wreckage, red like an opened pomegranate. His "reflection" could only last fifteen minutes, but it didn't seem like it would be a problem here. Actually, if he broke step, he could end it in ten seconds.

Then...

"Come on, what've I been tellin' ya?"

He heard a man's voice from one of the automobiles surrounding him.

"It'll take a lot more than this to crush that punk. You keep goin' easy on him 'cause he's a punk. That's why I told you to let me out first, remember?"

A man was kicked out of the still-open rear sliding door. After him, a tall man wearing a white robe lumbered out. His expression showed no signs of damage. Despite being a scientist, he had a tattoo on his face. His hands were clad in machined gloves. They had a dumb, long name—"micro-manipulators" or something. As the name implied, though, they were supposedly precision engineering tools that enabled delicate work on a micrometer scale.

"…"

Accelerator's brows knitted.

He knew this scientist.

"Pfft."

And as soon as he saw him, he burst out laughing.

"Gya-ha-ha-ha-ha!! What's with that suggestive entrance, eh, Kihara?! You don't seem like the kind of nerd to get scared of someone's face and look away!!"

Amata Kihara.

A man who, long ago, did the Ability Development on Academy City's strongest Level Five esper.

Which also meant he was the most talented Ability Development scientist in the entire city.

"Look, I didn't want to see your ugly face again, either. But I can't do anything about what the higher-ups tell me, eh? They were all *'It's an emergency'* and *'Do whatever it takes.'* So, uh, sorry, but do me a favor and let me crush you."

Accelerator ignored the man in white's bold front.

Everyone involved in researching Accelerator had been, without exception, afraid of his incredible abilities. In clearer terms, they'd never tried keeping him in one facility for more than two months. However lofty a scientist's ambitions were, the moment they saw someone with gifts far outrivaling their own, without exception, they would hide in the corner, quivering.

Amata Kihara was no more than one of those scientists.

Actually, Accelerator didn't even know any other types of scientist. Kikyou Yoshikawa being the one exception.

Kihara's shoulders drooped slightly in his lab coat. "Don't be like that. Who do you think discovered your powers for you?"

"Yeah? What was that? You talkin' to *me* about obligation and humanity? You one of those people who wants Accelerator to repay a favor? Shit, you're hopeless. And also..." Accelerator put his left index finger up to his temple and began twirling it around. "Go be insane somewhere else. I need more than my hands to count the number of scientists who fucked with my body. You think I was gonna remember you out of all of them, Passerby A? I think nothing of you, so would ya mind getting out of my sight?"

"You really are one annoying punk, you know that?" Kihara crossed his arms like he was worried about the cold. He chuckled and looked at Accelerator. "Man, I wanna kill you. I really, really want to kill you. To be honest with you, I've always wanted to beat that face of yours. I didn't before, since you were good research material, and you were still a brat, a fucking punk. What was I thinking? Knew I shoulda killed you back then. Man, I'm a failure. Ah-ha-ha, what the hell am I doing?"

He spread his arms out wide, his hands in those super-precision work gloves, reinforced with electrically contracted artificial muscles and small motors. Almost like he was welcoming back a lover.

Arms still spread, he began to approach Accelerator.

Recklessly.

The corners of the scientist's lips twisted.

And he said this:

"Which means it's time to die, you little shit."

He let fly a lean, gloved fist made of metal at Accelerator's face.

Accelerator, though, kept on smiling.

"What's this idiot thinking?" he muttered.

He would accept Amata Kihara's punch in that unguarded, wide-open stance of his, then break his arm as hard as he could and tie it into a slipknot.

*　　*　　*

Slam!!

The mechanical fist scraped off Accelerator's skin and rattled his skull.

"Gah...ergh...?!"

The unexpected strike had shocked his brain even more.

His electrode choker switch was flipped to "on."

His reflection was active.

Right now, he would have been able to blow himself up with a nuclear bomb and emerge unscathed.

And yet...

For some reason, his vector reflection wasn't working at all.

"And also," came Amata Kihara's voice in his shaky, wavering awareness. A disappointed voice—a scornful one. "*I don't think anything of you, either, you little shit.* Don't get all stuck up just 'cause you're a little powerful. I'll say it again. Who the hell *gave* you that bullshit ability? Come on, you remember now, don't you?"

"Agh..."

Before Accelerator could say anything, Amata came in with another punch.

The glove created a strange *gshhh* noise.

The strike came in like a hammer, from above to below. And once again, his reflection meant nothing. His head slugged, Accelerator collapsed onto the wet road surface. The modern-looking crutch fell out of his hand. The plastic bag from the pharmacy fell to the ground, and its contents scattered about.

"Let me crush you already. I've got important things to do, too. Don't have the time to fool around with the likes of you, got it?"

Kihara crushed the box of adhesive bandages underfoot.

The ones he'd bought for Last Order, specially made for children.

The cute-looking package, soiled with rainwater and mud.

"That ain't like you," Kihara said with a smirk. He rubbed his mechanical gloves together as if to check how he was doing. "Well, we'll recover *that* for you. You can rest easy as I squash you and use you to paint the wall. That'd be more like you, right?"

"…!!"

Heat rushed to Accelerator's head.

Amata Kihara had just said Accelerator wasn't his objective. And that he'd recover "that thing" who seemed to be near him all the time.

In other words, that was his goal.

He was telling him he'd drag the person he called "that" down into the bloody world where Accelerator and Kihara lived.

"Don't…you…," managed Accelerator, down on all fours.

Kihara and the men in black had gotten right up close to him—in other words, approached him defenselessly—to hold him down to the ground. They looked down at him. Accelerator glared.

His lips turned up slightly into a muddy smile.

"…Fuck with me, you pieces of traaaaaaaaaaaaaaash!!"

Boom!! went the wind as it swirled.

His ability was to manipulate vectors. If it had even a little strength, then regardless of its directionality, he could control it. And the wind—the atmospheric flows all around the planet—was no exception.

A local storm brewed.

The raging winds traveled at a controlled 120 meters per second; if it was a hurricane, it would have been M7 class, the highest there was. This violent wind force would even tear apart automobiles and house roofs. It was like a barrage of missiles.

"Kill them!" shouted Accelerator.

However—

"This won't do."

Beep.

There was a strangely dry sound, and as soon as he heard it, the violent wind mass Accelerator was controlling blew away. Like a balloon with a hole in it, the collected wind dispersed in every direction.

"?!"

He'd thought that would kill them for sure, but Kihara had gotten rid of it without so much as a concern.

He was beyond amazed—he was dumbfounded.

"So just die, will ya?"

Kihara picked up a nearby metal pipe and, with a *gong!!* smashed it into Accelerator's face.

He heard terrible cracking noises from his face. The immediate, pain-induced cry lost its exit and became a muffled groan. Once Kihara heard that, he tossed the pipe aside.

"Ogh…rgh…"

In his hazy consciousness, Accelerator thought.

He knew something similar to what was happening.

That guy, who had easily wiped out his Level Five power, which he thought absolute, using only the palm of his hand. The guy who destroyed his impenetrable ability to reflect dealt blow after heavy blow to his delicate body.

Could this be…?

"Did you…develop an ability…on yourself…?"

"Gya-ha-ha! Ah, no, that's not it. Why would I make myself into an experimental animal just to do that? We have lab rats for that. This ain't anything special. Even if you weren't using that insane power, I wouldn't break a sweat crushing you one-on-one. So why *am* I putting so much effort into crushing a pip-squeak like you, anyway?"

"…"

"Man, I'm in a good mood. Exterminating pests always puts me in one. These guys are doing well today, too," he said, opening and closing the fingers of his micro-manipulators.

Accelerator's shoulders gave a start.

This wasn't over.

He couldn't be crushed so easily here.

"Ohhh!!" roared Accelerator, controlling vectors to jump off the ground like a spring. He recklessly swung his arms. His modern-looking crutch fell away from his right arm, but he couldn't worry about that now.

He smashed five fingers at Amata Kihara.

The first time was a failure.

But the second time, his nails touched Kihara. He poured "energy" into them. Into the gloves he wore. He focused the vectors to a single point and turned the mechanical gloves into smithereens. Pieces flew all over.

"?!"

He could see Kihara's surprise past the debris flying into the air.

Accelerator shoved his open five fingers toward his face.

Now you're dead for sure, you shithead!!

He tore through the layer of machine parts and sent an attack certain to kill at the man's face.

However...

"Oh, I get it. You thought these gloves were the secret to my strength, didn't you?"

Kihara's voice was calm.

Just by turning his neck, he easily avoided Accelerator's strike, and on his face...

...was his usual grin.

"That ain't it! Gya-ha-ha! Sorry for getting your hopes up like that!!"

Slam!! He buried his fist in Accelerator's side.

The urge to vomit exploded within him, but even that was held down by force.

Kihara's gleeful voice pounded on his eardrums. "Ha-ha! *How long are you gonna keep pretending you're the strongest*, you pile of scrap?!"

Just as his body bent over in half, another punch flew at his head, which had come forward. He clattered to the road like a toy.

"Your *reflection* isn't a perfect wall."

Kihara slowly walked over to him.

Accelerator couldn't move.

"All you do is make vectors comin' at you the *opposite*. Then it's easy, yeah? All I gotta do to beat the shit out of you is pull my fist back the moment before it hits you. Like, right up to the edge."

He spoke like he was entertained.

He grinned like he was revealing the trick behind what he'd thought up.

"You're *reflecting a fist going away from you.* Basically means you're punching yourself! You get it, you masochistic pig?! Or is it too hard for your punk head to understand?!"

"!!"

Accelerator tried to get up, but Kihara's foot came at him first. The scientist stomped on him with the sole of his shoe, again and again. He crushed parts of Accelerator's body, tore away skin, and splattered blood that mixed with rainwater.

What...?

Accelerator could tell Kihara was using his ability against him. What he had no idea about, though, was what exactly was going on, whether such a thing was possible in reality rather than just on paper.

Either way, he decided reflection wouldn't cut it. "Gahhhh!!"

This time, he tried to make wind by controlling airflow vectors, but once again, it all blew away upon hearing a dry *beep.*

"It's the same thing," said Kihara. "Your ability is based on vector calculations. I just have to fuck them up. So, you can't control the wind, either. Control needs more complicated equations than just reflection. Same with program code. The more declarations you have, the more bugs are possible." He paused. "Of course, that goes for human interference, too. Essentially, I just gotta put a little sound wave in the air, and it'll jam your entire wind attack. As long as I emit sonic waves in directions that get into your equations' blind spots, you know?"

He then took out a cell phone...no, a phone strap hanging from it. It was made of a soft material that made a sound when pressing its button. That was all it took to block his power.

"Damn...it..."

"How's being stomped into the mud treating you? Your traits, your calculations, your personal reality—I know it all. How do you think I developed your ability?"

Thud!! Ka-thud!! Ger-thump!! A series of dull sounds.

A few drops of blood splashed onto Kihara's face.

He kicked and kicked until he was short of breath. Then, as

though it were the most hideous thing in the world, he scraped his red-stained shoe on the water-soaked road surface.

"Hmm? Pests really do take a long time to exterminate. Hey, you, get the thing out of the car. You know the one. Packed in the back, covered in dust."

He waved his hand out, and to answer, one of the injured men in combat clothing dragged himself into the backseat of a minivan. He took something out and gave it to Kihara—a heavy-looking toolbox large enough for a full-sized hammer or saw to fit into.

"Weapons are more effective when they're sloppy—or, perhaps, unsubtle. Kinda like how wooden chain saws are way more awesome than nonmetal assassination daggers."

Accelerator, still on the ground, couldn't say much. The raindrops continued to hit him as all he could manage was looking up at Kihara.

"Hey, Accelerator. You don't know what 'that thing' is, do you?"

Kihara grinned.

"The thing" could have only been the small girl.

"I mean, think about it. Before the Level Six shift project, it was, uh, the Radio Noise development project, yeah? Wasn't it even a little strange that they got the go sign as military production models? Why'd they take the third-place Railgun? Why not clone you instead? You were first place, right?"

"…"

"Why couldn't they clone you? Why'd they start up the project with third place? That's a hint, you know. A hint about something you don't even know the surface of."

"Hah," laughed Accelerator. "You piece of shit…," he muttered.

More than his lips were damaged. He felt blood seeping up from his throat and in between his teeth.

"…You understand even less about her than me, so I wouldn't get so fuckin' happy about saying random shit like that."

"Hmm?" Kihara grinned, grabbing the heavy-looking toolbox by the corners, checking to see how it felt in his hands. Happily, he said, *"How moving. She's pretty happy about it, too."*

Accelerator's heart skipped a beat.

His body wouldn't move.

Nevertheless, still on the ground, on all fours, he turned his head.

He looked one hundred meters away.

And there—

There was...

Arms held by men in black clothing...

...was a small girl, hanging there limply.

"Target recovered, I guess."

Amata Kihara's voice sounded distant to Accelerator's ears.

From down on the ground, he was looking at three people. Two were men, walking side by side, all in black. The third was Last Order, whom they were carrying like luggage. It was like they were holding a plastic bag with something heavy in it. The bottoms of her feet weren't in contact with the ground. Like a hanging rope, it was the tops of her feet limply hitting the ground instead.

From here, he couldn't see her face.

Like her limbs, her head hung like a branch in the wind, her bangs and the shadows hiding her face. And though it looked like a very painful position, she didn't budge an inch. She was probably out cold. If he got closer, he knew he'd be able to see signs of life in her young body.

As though his arm was tired, one of the men violently pushed Last Order to another one of his associates. Still her limbs hung helplessly, with no reaction from her at all.

Kihara grinned. "Ah, well, I guess it ain't listening anymore. I mean, our *real mission* was to take it alive, but can you really consider this living? I don't wanna be the one writing the apology here."

Fuck you, Accelerator tried to say.

She was still alive. She couldn't be dead. If Last Order was dead, it would affect him, too, since all the Sisters were doing the substitute calculations for him...at least, that's how he thought it worked.

Damn it, I've got no proof... Still down on the cold ground, he clenched his teeth. *If she dies, I don't know what kind of effects it would have! Never gonna test it, either, so how the fuck should I know?!*

Without a mind for the writhing Accelerator, the men holding the unconscious Last Order came over to him—or more accurately, toward the minivan.

Kihara said their objective was Last Order.

He didn't know where they planned on taking her, but if they threw her into that automobile, it was all over.

They'd drag her right back into that world stained in blood and darkness.

And then.

The probability she'd get out of there was likely zero.

Not gonna...happen...

Accelerator's fingers crawled across the rain-soaked ground.

He put his last iota of energy into his beaten body, then looked up and shouted.

"Last Ordeeeeeeeeeeeeeeeeeeer!!"

He thought he saw *the girl's shoulders move at being called.*

Still on the ground, he lifted his arm.

He couldn't rip Amata Kihara apart by controlling vectors. If he controlled the air and made a windstorm, Kihara would jam it with ease. If he used one of those methods of attack, he couldn't take down this man in the lab coat. Given the situation he was in, his main consideration wasn't crushing the man right now. Something else took priority.

Therefore...

"...!!" Accelerator bit down and slammed his hand down onto the damp asphalt.

Crash!! came the sound of destruction.

The extraordinary power blew the asphalt away, sending fragments in all directions and forcing Kihara back a bit.

He had less than a moment.

With the limited time he had, Accelerator's hand grabbed hold of the "wind" for sure this time.

Gales howled as he controlled the vectors.

"Shit!!" he heard Kihara swear. The buffeting wind lance pierced right by Kihara and toward the men in black holding Last Order.

Wind speed: 120 meters per second.

The hurricane could tear the roofs off automobiles and houses. It wrenched her small body out of the men's burly arms and flung her up and away. She crossed several ten-meter-high buildings, vanishing on the wind into the shadows of the scenery.

There was a strange *gubuh* from his throat.

Before he could think about holding it back, a chunk of blood came out of his mouth, and his face fell back to the rain-soaked road. The battery wasn't drained, but he couldn't devote enough mental energy to reflection anymore. Rainwater, mixed with blood and dirt, crept past the corners of his lips and onto his tongue.

"Ah, jeez, damn it," said Kihara in a relaxed tone. "She's not a golf ball. You can't just be launching people yards away. The flight distance is perfect. Who the hell do you think is gonna go get her now? I ain't doin' it."

"What should we do?" asked one of the men clad in black combat clothing, quietly seeking direction.

Kihara scratched his head with his right hand, which still had the remains of his glove on it. "Great...We split up, you know, into three groups. One group is on the main objective. Two stay with me. We got a lot to worry about—cleanup, the guys who went down over there, et cetera."

"If I may, our primary orders are to capture Last Order, so shouldn't the group assignments be—?"

"Oh?" Amata Kihara looked at his subordinate in blank amazement, then asked casually, "You're, uh, the one recruited to Hound Dog recently, right?"

"Well, not exactly—"

"It's fine, it's fine. Not tryin' to pry into your affairs or anything. No fun hearing about how some sweaty guy met his end. But you don't seem to know the rules, so let me explain them."

Kihara cleared his throat, seeming disinterested.

"You're a group of trash. You have no human rights. We can recruit as much trash as we need to replace you. If any of you get in the way of our *incredibly* important operation, I could kill you and it wouldn't matter. Get it now? You've already died once, yeah? I'll ask again. Am I clear?"

The sensation of raindrops sliding down his body disappeared.

Even the discomfort dissipated from the man in black who had been spoken to.

"We make the schedule ourselves here. Making me worry over some shitty little punks...It doesn't make sense, see? You gonna make me worry about a shit like you on top of that?"

A dreadful emotion from Kihara's body overtook their surroundings.

After seeing his subordinate unwittingly take a step back, he nodded simply. "Good, as long as we're clear. I'm actually *not* at the end of my rope now, so I'll take questions."

"...Y-yes, sir. About taking Last Order alive—with what happened..."

"I'm sure the punk's given that thought. Probably dropped her in a river somewhere."

"If she was, sir, considering she was passed out, she may be in danger of drowning..."

"Idiot. She'll wake up from the shock of hitting the water. Besides, I think she was at least conscious anyway. Just look around for anything that could've cushioned her fall and check nearby. She may be skilled at running away, but those bratty legs of hers can only take her so far. If that's all it takes for us to lose her, I'd bust a gut laughing at you."

"Yes, sir," came several voices at once.

Without much talk, with only eyes and fingers as signals, their lone team scattered onto the roads.

Kihara looked down to see what had become of Accelerator, who was lying in a puddle. "Now, then."

"Will we take him back as well, sir?"

"Nah, let's kill him. When I look at someone who makes a ton of work for me, I get all angry-like. No reason to capture him anyway. Didn't you see how annoying he is? Easiest thing with this kind of depressing, thinks-too-hard, self-righteous asshole is to kill him on the spot."

He spoke like he was watching a caterpillar on a tree.

One person in combat gear drew his pistol, but Kihara shook his head. Dealing with Accelerator's reflection was accomplished by "pulling back" his limbs in an odd way. One couldn't do the same with a bullet.

This, of course, was a way of attacking only possible because Kihara had been the one to directly develop Accelerator's ability. Even if he explained the trick, Kihara was probably the only one with a high enough combat level to pull off such delicate, split-second timing.

Kihara squatted and lifted the toolbox in his hands overhead.

It was far heavier than a hammer. It was a more primal, blunt weapon.

He aimed for Accelerator's wrecked face as if to crush an empty can on the ground.

"Nice surprise there, punk, but now you gotta kill me. Dunno if you were tryin' to make a crazy comeback or what, but we'll get that thing in a cage before ten minutes are up."

"...Shut up," spat Accelerator.

"Oh?" Kihara's eyes widened. He probably didn't think Accelerator was actually awake.

"Piece of shit. You'd...never understand."

"That so? All right, I'm killin' you now. Those your last words?" Kihara barked out a laugh. "Have fun bein' a shit stain on the road."

"Damn," muttered Accelerator without letting it show.

Kihara was right. At this rate, they'd catch Last Order. She had some ability to run away, but she was at an overwhelming disadvantage.

What was Yomikawa doing? Wasn't Yoshikawa coming here with a gun? He knew the answer. Of course not. Nothing so convenient could ever happen. If someone else showed up to resolve everything, like puzzle pieces, whenever he ran into a situation he needed to get himself out of, nobody would ever stray from the path of righteousness. Universal brotherhood. Everyone smiles, everyone's happy. Incredibly warm illusions, but nothing like that could ever come to pass.

...Someone..., thought Accelerator despite that. *I need some luck*

here, a lucky illusion…I'll give you the credit, if that's what you want. Don't even care if you laugh your ass off as he stomps on me.

Lying on the rain-soaked ground, an instant away from his skull being smashed in, the very picture of ugliness.

Someone, I don't care who, get her…

His wish would never reach.

The toolbox mercilessly swung down to hammer into him.

An instant before it did…

"…What are you doing over there?"

"Eh?" Kihara's raised arms froze in midair.

The guys wearing combat clothing turned around to where the voice came from.

It was not even twenty meters away. It'd probably come from one of the smaller side roads all of a sudden. On the nighttime streets under the drizzling rain, standing there with an umbrella up, was a person, illuminated by a streetlight, radiating dully.

The person had long, silver hair reaching down to the waist, white skin, and green eyes. She wore a showy nun's habit, its white fabric embroidered with gold like a teacup. But there were safety pins stuck to it all over, making her outfit very unbalanced. In her hands was a calico that didn't look like it belonged in this strained, tense world.

Accelerator, on the ground, remembered.

Remembered her.

Remembered her name.

2

"Damn it, Index. As soon as I found you, you disappeared again. Where on earth did you go?"

Touma Kamijou muttered to himself as he looked back and forth, to and fro.

After the last schools let out, the underground mall didn't have many people in it. As always, it was a world of bare white fluorescent lights from which a person couldn't tell day or night or the weather outside, but given the differences in population and music played inside stores, one could, little by little, feel time passing.

Kamijou, for his part, was still stuck trying to figure out why Index had fled home in the first place.

Incidentally, their conversation upon meeting had gone something like this.

"Academy City is complicated and annoying, and I don't really get how it's laid out. That's why it took so long to search for you, Touma. Well, anyways, let's go home, okay?"

"Wait, why did you come all the way here looking for me, anyway? …Actually, I bet it's the usual *I'm hungry* thing."

"Touma, you're stupid!!"

"*Gowah!* Did you just bite me out of nowhere?!"

"If you think I only do anything when I'm hungry, then that's a big mistake!!"

"But isn't it more unusual for you to do anything for some other reason?!"

"Touma, you don't have enough consideration. The white-haired person I met when I came here was a lot more considerate. He even let me eat hamburgers without asking what was wrong. You should be more kind like him, Touma."

"Yeah, yeah. I don't have anything to do with guys like that, after all. Oh, did you remember to thank him? You didn't get anything else from him, did you?"

"Mgh. I know how to properly thank someone. But now that I think of it, I think he lent me this."

"What? That's just a packet of tissues."

"Oh no! What is that person going to do now without this cutting-edge necessity? He must be worried! T-Touma, I have to go give this back real quick!!"

"Huh? But they're just tissues. Blowing your nose in them and giving them back is what'll worry him— Hey, don't just sprint off like that! Listen to me! Index!!"

Calling her on a cell phone would have made things fast, but he knew hers was shut off as always. He wandered through the underground mall, peeking into fast-food places, but he couldn't find her. She was looking for someone, so maybe she decided he wasn't down here and went above ground. On the other hand, maybe she didn't have a reason at all—the sister got lost in Academy City pretty often for someone with perfect memory.

Kamijou climbed up the stairs and left the mall.

"Huh?!" he muttered suddenly, looking at the sky. "It's raining..."

The drizzling raindrops had dampened the road, making it black. Now that it was September, it was also understandably colder out than before.

...I didn't leave the futon out to dry, did I? Did Index close the windows before leaving? Well, I'll have to start by finding her, he thought, glancing at the sky, covered with thick clouds, as he continued walking for some reason or other. It was raining, but maybe it wasn't bad enough to need an umbrella. He was close to the dorm anyway. He bought a cheap umbrella every time he went home in the rain, so there was a whole rack of them in his room now. It made him not want to go back into the mall to purchase another.

...Man, I feel like there's a lot of Anti-Skill officers out today...

Maybe it was the time; maybe it was the weather. The darkened streets were unusually empty of students. There were only Anti-Skill officers around.

They were wandering about, decked out in defensive outfits of laminated plastic and shock-resistant urethane foam. It had probably been waterproof originally, but he felt bad for the ones patrolling without umbrellas in this somewhat chilly rain.

Hmm. Maybe if you're out walking around too late they start directing people. I know how to slip past them...but Index doesn't. And she'll just make the conversation worse, then get directed to the station.

He decided to get her and bring her home before anything annoying happened and was about to look away from Anti-Skill, when...

*   *   *

There was a strange *plop*.

"...?"

Kamijou stopped.

An Anti-Skill officer in full armor standing right nearby, without any indication, had crumpled to the ground facedown. The puddles on the road began to overtake the officer. And still, he didn't move. Waterproof was one thing, but that wasn't a normal reaction. Even idiots didn't jump into pools with raincoats on.

...Is he out cold?

Kamijou didn't know how comfortable their official gear was.

But if it was like a cartoon character costume, the officer might dehydrate or get a fever. It was a little cold for Kamijou, but there were plenty of possibilities for the officer with all the thick armor on that wouldn't apply to him.

Not good.

Kamijou's eyes darted around.

No normal students around, but plenty of Anti-Skill officers.

Still, he went toward the fallen one for now.

And then.

This time, from somewhere else.

Kamijou's ears heard a *blat*. The sound of someone falling. And not only once, either. One, then another, until the thuds transformed into one long sound.

"Wha...?"

He looked around, doubting his eyes, then froze.

Every one of the officers patrolling the night streets had fallen. It wasn't like anything had hit them; they all just kind of dropped. And they weren't even trembling, much less moving their fingertips. He could tell even from far away. They were completely out cold.

"Hey...What the hell?! Hey!!"

This time, he ran in a panic.

He went for the first officer to go down. The figure facedown in the puddle seemed to be male. Even in this state, though, Kamijou decided he could still suffocate, so he moved the man out of the puddle for the time being and flipped him faceup.

His body was hefty.

Whether it was his equipment or his actual body weight, he couldn't tell.

What about the others?

He ran about but found nobody who seemed to be suffocating. He'd have carried them all into the underground mall if he could have, but he didn't have the strength for it. All that weight would be like carrying around sandbags.

Calling for someone would have been a challenge, too.

The road they were on was fairly large, but Academy City was essentially a collection of school towns. Save for a few faculty-oriented entertainment districts, most of the city shut down when the sun set. The only stores with their lights on were convenience stores and restaurants with the permission to operate late into the night. The last trains and buses were done, and not a single car sat on the six-lane road. It didn't get more discouraging than this. And in reality, he couldn't see any signs of commotion from so many people collapsing. It seemed better to abandon any hope of someone nearby doing something about this.

This is originally the kind of situation Anti-Skill is for, too…

Kamijou peered into the face of the officer.

Nonmetal pieces covered most of his body, so unless he took them off, he wouldn't know the extent of the man's injuries. At least his clothing wasn't dyed crimson or anything. He decided to imitate the thing from movies and TV dramas and put his hand to the man's neck. The pulse of life he felt gave a reassuring signal to his fingertips. When he put his palm up to his neck, he could tell the man was breathing stably.

No threat to his life…at least, that's how it looked.

But if the man wasn't injured, what had caused this?

Anesthetic gas…? No…

That wouldn't explain why only Kamijou was safe.

Either way, leaving it to his amateurish judgment would be bad.

All he could do was call an ambulance.

Kamijou took out his phone, then dialed a three-digit number to connect to a call center. He was nervous just pressing the call button to an emergency number like this, but it wasn't the first time he had reported something. His thoughts were rather muddled, but he managed to explain the situation.

He snapped his cell phone closed.

In order to put it back in his pocket, he stood back up.

And then...

"*...Zzz...zzh...*"

There was a noise at his feet. He dropped his gaze. The fallen Anti-Skill officer still wasn't moving even a fingertip. A radio was near his neck, though, which was where the static came from.

"*Zzz-sshhhh-zzz*...broken into. I repeat...*sshhhzzzzzz!!*...Gate breach confirmed! The intruder is entering the city—isn't anyone listening? Our unit is taking another attack from unknown— *Gwah?!*"

Bss-shoo!! came a noise like a CRT television turning off.

The sound came from a wireless device. The person speaking must have been an officer somewhere else. The desperate words worried him, but now only an even static *zzzz* was coming from the square device. At a glance, it looked like an unadorned cell phone, but it probably worked totally differently. He didn't feel like messing with it.

What was that...? thought Kamijou, looking away.

He went over the static-filled words that came over the radio.

...An intruder.

Which would mean someone came into Academy City from outside. It wasn't clear whether that was related to the officers nearby going down like this. In either case, though, Kamijou's thoughts were *Hope Index is all right...*

Not every enemy of the city was someone from the sorcery side, and even if it was a sorcerer, no rule said they would all go after Index. Still, she was the first thing he thought about, anyway.

This is bad, he thought, switching gears. It seemed best to find her soon to make sure she was safe, just in case.

And then...

"?"

Plop. A soft impact rolled through Kamijou's side.

Someone seemed to have hit him…but the point of contact was weirdly low. Not around his chest, but lower, around his waist.

He glanced down.

The culprit was a small child. She was over a full head shorter than him. Probably around ten years old. Her brown hair just barely reached down to her shoulders.

Right, her name was… "Last Order, right?"

He heard a moan in response.

Her answer was muffled because she'd pushed her little face into Kamijou's shirt. Rather than hitting him, it was more like she'd come up and hugged him. She was trembling all over, and her lack of body heat from the rain hitting her made its way through his shirt. She was far too soaked to have been out in this drizzle for a little while.

What happened? he wondered.

"Help…"

Still gripping the bottom of his shirt, Last Order looked up.

Her eyes were bright red and bloodshot, and clear liquid was dripping down one cheek.

Even in the cold rain, he could immediately tell that one drop apart.

She was—

She shouted.

"I'm begging you, save him…! pleads Misaka pleads Misaka!!"

Two girls crossed, connected to the two espers.

Their completely parallel paths should never have allowed them to meet.

But at the moment, their paths converged…

…The true story began, with Academy City as its stage.

INTERLUDE FIVE

People slammed to the ground, one by one.

In the cold downpour, without resistance, without noise, without blood, without screams—only the sound of people collapsing traveled through the dark, dark streets that night. Every one of them an adult wearing shock-resistant armored clothing. The bald streetlights illuminated their firearms in puddles with glares.

They were Anti-Skill officers, tasked with the security of Academy City.

The fallen didn't move.

Not even a fingertip.

But near them could be heard short, quick footsteps.

As though weaving between the victims, lying quietly on the wet road, was the slender silhouette of a woman moving languidly across the rainy streets.

The woman under the streetlights didn't have an umbrella. The thin, threadlike rain struck her slim, young-looking figure. She wore a woman's kirtle, a kind of clothing that gave birth to the dress. She also had a thin leather belt on her waist, along with detachable sleeves running from her wrists to her upper arms. Think of it as a glorified version of what bank and mail clerks wear. On her head was a simple hood, hiding all her hair.

If one had some interest in history or archaeology, they might have pinned it as the common garb of a French citizen around the fifteenth century.

However, because its main color was a gaudy yellow, one couldn't call it archetypical, either.

A subtle jingling of metal could be heard.

It came from the piercings in the woman's face. She had holes in her ears, obviously—but also her nose, lips, and even her eyelids. Her lips opened, and she stuck out her tongue, letting a chain fall from it. A small necklace-like chain linked to the opening in her tongue and reached down to waist level. A cross-shaped charm hung from it.

It had all been done in the knowledge that she was ruining her face.

In Crossism, "metal piercing" held deep meaning. Originally, the Son of God had been pierced with nails and lances when he was martyred. By carefully selecting the places to pierce, it was possible to freely construct certain spells, too.

"Hmm."

The woman, face fully pierced, looked around her, then kicked a wireless radio at her feet into the air. She caught the spinning, square device with one hand. The feeling of mud made her frown slightly.

She twirled the radio in her hand like a pistol, then brought her mouth near the microphone.

As if whispering into someone's ear, she spoke.

"Helllloooo, Aleister?"

With a buzz of static, the voice of a worried Anti-Skill officer came back. But the woman ignored everything he said, as if addressing somebody who couldn't have been listening.

"I bet you've wormed into all these regular lines. I'd really appreciate it if you talked to me already."

Bzzt came the sound of a switch flipping.

The sound quality immediately cleared up.

"What is it?"

"Oh, if you really want to know, I guess I can tell you."

"Just to confirm, you didn't actually think I'd fall for a taunt like that, did you?"

"Sure did. I've already stomped on three General Board faces, and you wouldn't respond to that." She spun the radio around and around in her hand. Her face held a hint of disappointment. "There's only twelve on the General Board, right?"

"We can replace as many of them as we need."

"My, how scandalous."

"I have many ways to deal with it."

"You know, Aleister. I've been thinking. Maybe you don't actually exist. Maybe you're just a 3-D image, or maybe you just put a weird machine in your corpse and use that to move."

"Dreamlike assertions. You're no scholar—you're suitable as an innovator."

"The collective will of the General Board is hidden behind your opinions...or so I thought, but huh, guess I was wrong. You don't seem flustered at all.

"Maybe I'll just crush a few more of 'em, then," she muttered.

The radio remained silent.

It was like he'd said it would take more than that to affect him.

"Well, whatever. You know my name?"

"Perhaps. I do make it a point to investigate the likes of rebels and thieves."

"God's Right Seat."

Smoothly.

The woman named the strongest, most deeply rooted organization on the sorcery side.

A single name, sunken into the depths of the dark of the dark of the dark of the dark of the dark of the dark of the dark of the dark of the world's largest religious order, the Roman Orthodox Church. Even among its two billion followers, only a handful knew the name. As for those who did know it, if they were judged "unworthy of knowing," they were immediately put to death. The term held that much secrecy.

But Aleister replied smoothly, too.

With no sign of emotion.

"Well, now. A group labeled terrorists had a name like that, didn't they?"

"Hmm."

"This seems a little reckless for a PR stunt."

"Feign ignorance if you want. Just make sure you don't regret not begging for your life now, when all this is over."

"You aren't making light of this city, are you?"

"Oh my. You don't have a grip on how your own city's doing right now? Communication problems already? Well, please excuse me. You see, I can't even count the number of enemy soldiers I've made a mess of. Ha-ha. Even the operator's down?"

"..."

"Sixty percent. Seventy percent. Eighty percent might be pushing it. Whatever. It'll be one hundred percent soon enough. 'Anti-Skill' and 'Judgment,' were they? It's because you try to defend yourself with such cheap labor that I can just waltz in and detach your head. You must at least know you're done for, right?"

"Heh."

"?"

"If you think you've broken through Academy City's defenses, then ignorance truly is bliss. *You don't understand the true form of this city.*"

"Really, now?"

"What I mean is this—you aren't the only one with something still hidden. Of course, we might defeat you before you find out what mine is."

"Whatever it is, I'll crush anyone who stands in my way. It's been a predetermined rule since I was born."

It seemed like they were exchanging words, but each was only talking *at* the other, saying what they wanted.

The woman looked at the mud-covered radio.

"I am Vento of the Front. The ultimate weapon out of two billion."

And last, she said this:

"I will destroy everything in this single night. You, Academy City, the Imagine Breaker, the Index—all of it."

With that, the woman calling herself Vento crushed the radio in her bare hand.

The *person*, Aleister, was in a room of a building with no windows.

A cylindrical life-preserving device sat in the middle of the rectangular space as though enshrined there, and the person floated upside down within. The red fluid it was filled with permeated Aleister's body through the mouth and nose, continuously acting on every single cell.

There was normally no real illumination here—only the countless lights like stars, created by the mechanical indicator lights completely covering all four walls of the spacious room. But right now, blinking red warning lights were intermittently brightening up the vast space.

As mentioned before, this room had no equipment to illuminate it.

The red light was actually the amalgamation of countless errors displayed on computer monitors. It went to show how much of an emergency the entire Academy City area found itself in right now.

Because of just one sorcerer.

Because of one of the God's Right Seat.

Academy City, which hadn't been swayed even by the Croce di Pietro.

"..."

In less than an hour, almost 70 percent of the Anti-Skill officers upholding the peace of Academy City had been laid to waste. As far as the life signs told Aleister, none were dead. But if the city fell before they awoke, it would be impossible for them to regroup. Damage reports and reinforcement requests flooded in from all over, but it would be a great bother to answer every single one of them.

The city was on the verge of death.

And yet—

Despite that—

The *person* Aleister wore only a smile on his lips.

An inexplicable smile—one that could apply to any emotion and yet applied to none at all.

"Fascinating," he whispered. "So incredibly fascinating. This is why I cannot stop living. A chance to use *it* has finally appeared. It is too soon…but my plans are holding things up. Irregularities are the greatest form of entertainment."

He toyed with that emotion, rolling it over his tongue. At the same time, he delivered countless control orders to his instruments from within his life-preservation machine. Touching one of the wireless devices, he flung frequencies and secret codes at it to connect to those who crawled like worms through the darkness of Academy City.

"Hound Dog—Amata Kihara," said Aleister.

After receiving a curt response, he ordered something extra.

"School District *i*, the Five Elements Society…The involuntary diffusion fields. It's a bit early, but we will use Hyouka Kazakiri to crush 'them.' I don't mind if you need to take off her limbs. As soon as you capture the fleeing serial number 20001, bring her to the point I specify—quickly and courteously."

Then, with a smile, he said:

"I've waited with bated breath for so long for showtime to begin."